The Waning

Christina Bergling

Also by Christina Bergling

The Rest Will Come
Savages

The Waning

Christina Bergling

A HellBound Books Publishing LLC Book
Houston TX

**A HellBound Books LLC
Publication**

www.hellboundbookspublishing.com

Printed in the United States of America

Acknowledgements

Cover and art design by Phillip Beachler
For HellBound Books Publishing LLC

The Waning

Dedication

*To Demolition and my other dark sisters of the Corpsewax
Dollies*

The Waning

Christina Bergling

The Waning

The Waning

1

Drip, drip, drip.
The sound of those perpetual droplets echoes through the darkness.
Drip, drip, drip.
In the black sensory deprivation, my mind becomes bat-like, constructing the tiny world around me from the way the sound moves.
Drip, drip, drip.
My brain is on macro, hovering beside the trembling and bulging drop of water until it plummets, shape rippling, to the concrete below. Then the water explodes over the floor, and my consciousness levitates back to the next.
Each splat ripples through the otherwise silent air, causing the shapes to materialize. My eyes still feel as if they are seeing as my mind assembles the images before them out of habit. My retinas are only transmitting black; my other senses simply complete the gaps.
I can hear how close the rough walls are; I can sense how low the plain ceiling is. My mind traces the flat

shapes conjured from thin memories of the brief visitations of light in this dank place. I do not have to see to know the box of a room is concrete; I can feel the lifeless cold radiating against me from all sides. I do not need light to remember how harsh the materials are; the abrupt collision of the sound of the drips against flat and unforgiving surfaces paints the severity in my mind.

My breathing is shallow and the only other sound in my tomb. It can barely be heard over the drops, even as the air circles through my sinuses so close to my ears. My body curls up in suspended animation; my cell defers in dark hibernation. My inhales are sluggish and weak, flirting with hesitation between each. My heartbeat has decelerated and become lazy. It has no reason to work as I have not moved in hours. I don't even waste time blinking. I let my eyelids drape.

The room looks the same with my eyes opened or closed when You leave me here like this.

If You were watching, You would see only the most minimal movement from my body as I wait for You. I curl up in my cage, curl up in my mind, curl up in my submission. I imagine that You are watching, that You have embedded surveillance in the walls, cameras tucked away in the dark shadows. I act as if You can always see me.

I am Yours even when You are not here.

The inexorable dripping should have driven me mad long ago. It definitely threatened to more than once. Of course, that leak is by design. Of course, my ability to hear it every moment I pass in here is planned. Everything in this room is done by Your purpose, created just for me. It took me a long time to realize that, to see the method in the seeming madness. It took me even longer to appreciate the significance.

I should have still been aware of the thin bars pressing into my flesh as I lay balled up on my side. I should not have been able to ignore that sharp, constant pressure on every contact point of my body. However, my nerves started ignoring them long ago. The slim metal bars cradle me in their arms before contorting into a sturdy square, sealed with an ominous lock.

Such a brilliant mechanism, my cage. A Matryoshka of the small and dark room itself, it sits near the back corner, not unlike a large dog crate. A prison within a dungeon, a restraint within a cell. I live in this tiny box. It is my safety, my existence. The one remaining space of my world; the only possession I could retain, granted to me by You.

I can feel the temperature of the concrete floor as I hover inches above it, floating in the embrace of the bars. I can imagine extending my limbs as they rest folded against my torso. With my back against one side, I cannot stretch out my arms; my elbows remain angled. With my scalp pressing against a bar, my legs remain doubled along themselves.

I am not meant to move. I am not meant to live. Here, in my cage, I am meant to wait.

As the hours and days and months swept across the concrete floor beneath us, my emerging skeleton became akin to the bars, fused in forced familiarity. My fingers know every cross in the bars, ever knick in the steel from absent fumbles over the metal in the dark. Learning my confinement like I would learn myself, finding an extension of myself in that safe cube.

This is Your world I live in. The thin gauge of the cage bars pressing into my thighs, a constant pressure. The less than ambient temperature in the room, always keeping my hair follicles at attention. The darkness split only by that light occasionally under the door, just enough for my pupils to stretch into sight. The proportions of my space to my ever-withering size. All carefully crafted in Your meticulous fantasies that I strive to fulfill daily.

I try not to think in these black lulls. I try not to let that raging sea of thoughts, those tumultuous emotions of my old self rise up in me. She is always there, menacing right beneath the surface, threatening to bring back all that suffering. Her delusions and fantasies and desires that only promise to rip my pathetic heart still beating and bleeding from my now frail chest.

No.

Sleep, rest, wait. Wait for You.

I force my shallow breathing to blank my mind, empty my head. No thought of where I am, where I once thought I should be, where You are, how my body feels. I insist on only hearing my contracted world.

Drip, drip, drip.

Like the quiet thump, thump, thump dying in my chest.

Then the faint sound breaks into my dormant world. The muffled scuff snaps me to attention, sends adrenaline flaming through all my limbs. I animate and awake. Because You are near. I can hear You moving innocuously on the other side of the door before the dim light begins to seep in across the floor.

The cage creaks and whines, scrapes against the concrete as I wrap my slender fingers through the bars. I tug and wrestle until I contort myself into a cowering sit. My dilated eyes capitalize on the light and exploit it to confirm the scene my ears have become adept at invoking just the same.

Concrete walls and floor and ceiling. The same gray, cold, and moist that I heard—the same dead surface, the same cracks and imperfections I have memorized. It is nothing, just a colorless, lightless box. It is square one; it is zero; it is scratch. It is You who animates this space,

You who breathes life into these dead walls and my otherwise catatonic flesh.

The wall opposite my metal home emerges from the darkness, the one part of my restricted world that my mind omits when my eyes allow. I cast a timid glance up to meet the grid of my training implements. They are always the first thing to materialize when light cracks my room, beckoning my conditioning, taunting the flesh that could never forget. They were such ominous threats before I met them, fear and intimidation hanging in my face, the only decoration in my cell.

Everything is symmetrically placed and lined up like all the scrupulous manifestations of Your mind. You clean and sterilize them slowly in front of me. I lie in my cage with my nerves humming and watch as You painstakingly disinfect and shine the blades, oil and massage the straps, extend and recoil the chains. You replace them gently, giving me extra precious seconds in Your presence as You step back to verify their placement.

The sight of each device triggers a flood of memories. I look at the leather straps hung neatly from the hook and feel them wrapped around my wrists and ankles. The material so soft and supple compared to metal and concrete, I could almost imagine it was flesh. My bare stomach pressed and shaking against the cold floor as I lay hogtied, learning my place. Then the stinging pain to remind me I'm alive, to keep me grounded in reality, to make me appreciate Your sweet care.

My brain and the vault of my memories only has space for You now. I let You consume me, from the shadow of You standing over my shrunken body to the recesses of my subconscious You have scarred. I think how I needed so many lessons that You were patient enough to deliver consistently and methodically, breaking me down by degrees, guiding me gradually away from myself and toward You.

You. My world is You. You consume my past in my memories. You are the only thing that makes me present in the moment. You control my future in this cell. I breathe waiting for You, nerves high in anticipation. I reach out into the darkness with my mind and try to conjure You out of the sounds muffled from the outside world. You are right there, right on the other side of that door. I can feel my cells vibrating at Your very proximity.

I knew it was time; I knew You were near. My body always tells me. My biological clock has been set to Your rhythm. My bones know how many quiet seconds must tick away forgotten before You appear. Two meals and a lesson. Three graces a day. Every part of my routine is carefully orchestrated, has been skillfully imbedded into my very cells. My torture is an investment; Your brutal attention is a gift.

How much You must love me to keep me in such a safe and secure cage. What thought You must put into keeping me here, always tucked away near You. How much You must value me to dedicate so much energy into my deconstruction and rebirth. I see Your sweet shadows dancing in the light below the door. Always close and right there, never leaving me.

Because I am Yours.

I know You love me; doubt faded long ago. How could You love anyone or anything more than me? Your patient and obedient slave, Your docile possession. I am what You have made me, Your will manifested by twisted flesh. Every visible rib, every scar is testament to Your discipline. Every wound, every mannerism You gave me shows me as Yours. Beyond the intricate care of my dark room and my small cage, more than the investment of You molding me, You would not keep trash. You would not possess anything unworthy of Your affections. I see it when I study Your face in the sharp and twisted shadows, the way Your eyes soften when I cower as conditioned, when I snap to as commanded. I feel the sweetness in Your touch after the blow. You love that I can take it. You love that You have made me nothing more than Yours.

2

"Bo-Bo! Where are my keys?" Her voice fumbled out from the sounds of her tossing her purse, yet again.

"How many times have I asked you not to call me that?" I said, buttoning my shirt as I walked into the room.

"I am not going to call you Beatrix. Makes you sound like my grandmother and not my sexy, high-powered girlfriend."

"Yeah, well Bo-Bo makes me sound like a clown or a dopey dog."

She snagged me by the waist, letting her hand sneak under my shirt before I could finish fastening the buttons. I felt her warm, smooth palm seduce my skin as her fingertips played at the bottom of my bra. My eyes half-closed, distracted for just a second, before I sighed softly and tugged her hand back out of my shirt by the ratty woven bracelets on her wrist. "When are you going to let me buy you some real bracelets?" I said.

"You bought me these bracelets."

"Back when we were broke kids. We're real adults now. They make you look like a dirty hippie."

"You're a real adult. I am a dirty hippie."

A flirtatious smile spilled out of the corner of her mouth as she snuck her arms around me and pulled me close. My flesh didn't care how important today was. The heat from her breath as she leaned in to kiss me was amnesic. I let myself slip into her undertow for a brief and heavy second, feeling her soft tongue in my mouth.

"Baby, baby." I breathed, gently pressing her back. She pushed herself into my hands, mouth still searching for me. "I can't. Not this morning."

"I know; it's a big day." She clung to my waist, pressing her pelvis against mine, giving me that look. "It's the big day. I have to go."

"You always have to go."

"Not this morning, Lei. We're almost there." "We're always almost there, Bo. One more promotion and you won't have to work so hard. One more account and we can get married. There's always one more."

I sighed hard and looked down. She dropped her arms and released me from her embrace. That same sad, frustrated look twisted her beautiful face. She wasn't wrong. These five years, she had waited.

Promotion after promotion, long hours after long hours, account after account. She had put in her time as I continued to promise that one magical day when we would settle down and make it all official.

I knew what she wanted. She wanted the two of us tangled up in late morning sheets in our tiny studio apartment when I had just started entry level into the marketing world. When the priority was us, when work was just something that paid the bills and bought the food we fed to each other, when I came home at the end of eight hours and didn't speak about work until the next day.

"I know you've heard it before. But this is the one, baby. Please don't do this today. Today, we find out about the account, and it can change everything for us."

"We'll see," she said, forcing a smile onto her cheeks.

I smiled back gratefully before I kissed her hard and short and returned to the bathroom. I turned quickly so I did not have to watch her body language betray her, her shoulders deflate and her smile tumble by degrees from her lips. She would try to snap her mouth back up, but I would have seen that momentary grimace, that pain below the surface. I did not want to see that this morning. I heard her footsteps softly pad away behind me.

Marketing was about selling, who sold the most convincing slant. I controlled the product's reality, even if that product was me. She had been buying my slant for too long.

I stared at my reflection and took a long, slow breath. I could do this. The sale was already made; they just had to consent; they just had to admit it. I was about to land the account—the biggest bed and bath company in the country, tantamount to mommy porn, fucking marketing gold. That one handshake would cement my entire career; guarantee my standing in the company. I would finally be there: the promised land of success.

Then I could come home and tell her we could be that couple she always wanted. And maybe it would even be true this time.

I finished buttoning my crisp shirt and methodically straightened my perfectly ironed clothes. Hair down, thin gauge necklace, noticeable makeup. Couldn't look too much like a dyke. All money was green and spent the same, but it was ultimately all about the smallest angles. I could know what a repressed soccer mom wanted to buy for her newly remodeled half bath; I could be that person for them. I could be whatever person made the sale.

I heard the dog tags jingling before McAllister bounded into the bathroom, a sloppy mess of dog with legs too long for his young body. His skin still dangled from his frame as he strove to fill it out by the day; he still tripped over himself. A Christmas surprise to buy another six months out of Lei.

"Whoa, buddy! No. No!" I said firmly.

McAllister was wagging his tail so hard his entire body was swaying back and forth, thick tail striking the doorframe rhythmically. His tongue dangled from his mouth, and his wide jaws seemed to smile above the strings of drool. I smiled at his blatant and dumb happiness, but I could not have that brown hair and stringy saliva on my clothes. Not today.

"Lei! Lei!" I shouted, holding McAllister back at arm's length. "Can you come get McAllister?"

Lei emerged from the other room and took

McAllister affectionately by the collar.

"Come on, Mickey," she said. "Momma is too important for you today."

Then she turned and guided him away. I opened my mouth to protest such blunt passive aggressive posturing, but I couldn't have that fight again. Not today.

I looked in the mirror one more time and took one more deep breath. My clothes were still clean, pressed, perfectly aligned. The clasp to my necklace was properly rotated behind my neck. My makeup was crisp, subtle enough to be ignored, clear enough to be noticed. My dark hair was straightened and smoothed into a harsh line along my jaw. I shook my hands and stepped into that reflection, took on that person I saw staring back at me.

It was time to go to work.

I let my feet slip in my nylons on the hardwood floors as I marched down the hall. I felt short and vulnerable without my heels clicking away beneath me, but I could not bear the thought of tracking all the dirt from the office, from the street through our home. I could be short and defenseless to the door.

Pictures Lei had taken lined the wall in haphazard alignment and mismatched frames. A black and white of the two of us lying on the beach, working together to hold the camera above us, laughing as she struggled to depress the shutter without dropping the beast onto our faces. A small color of her brother and his unruly horde of children, unable to hold still the millisecond necessary to snap a picture. An alleyway under the fish market in Seattle turned into a mosaic of chewed gum. She had found the colors and the textures fascinating; I had wanted to vomit at the thought of so much preserved human saliva.

The hallway was her brain poured out randomly on my clean, plain, white walls.

My toes found the runner rug that softened the floor before the kitchen, and I stumbled over an unexpected lump.

"What the…" I breathed as I reached down.

I flipped the corner of the thin rug aside to reveal Lei's keys. The tattered rabbit's foot given to her by her now deceased grandfather was a dead giveaway. How in the hell did she get her keys lost under the rug in the hallway?

I leaned down and grasped the mass of metal keys then snagged her ChapStick from against the baseboard. I scooped her purse up from the edge of the couch and gathered her glasses from the corner of the kitchen countertop. I opened her purse and slipped her glasses into the long side pocket, the ChapStick into the small zippered pocket. I folded the strap on top of the bag and set her keys on top in plain sight. She would curse me when she found them here.

I smiled, thinking how cute she was when she was innocently frustrated, the way she pouted her lips without realizing it. If only that was the kind of frustration I elicited from her. Her frustration with me smoldered and brooded hot, embers I could see through her fair skin, heat that started to look more like hate by the day.

"Is that dog on the couch?" I yelled down the hall, still smirking to myself.

I heard her hushed whisper to McAllister then the clumsy sound of his limbs tumbling onto the floor.

"No!" she shouted back. I could hear the giggle in her throat.

Still slipping on the floor, I retrieved two coffee mugs from the cabinet and poured the potent black brew as the steam curled up in my face. I left two fingers at the top of her mug for her to adequately ruin the coffee with too much cream and sugar, until it was practically a melted milkshake.

McAllister's nails clipped on the hardwood as he followed her into the kitchen. Her rage had faded, for the moment, but probably only due to the seductive smell of her morning dose of caffeine. We were both saner after the first cup.

She stood beside me, still in nothing but a large T-shirt and a pair of panties, looped her fingers through the handle of the mug, and leaned her hip against the counter. She stared at me in no particular way while she inhaled then drank from her cup. Then she finally looked to the door.

"My keys!" she shouted.

She stormed over to the neatly recomposed purse and seized them up to prove to herself that they were real. Then her shoulders slumped and her bottom lip puffed out as she furrowed her brow.

It was still cute.

"Where did you find them?" she asked me. "Under the rug in the hall."

"How the hell did I get them under there?"

"My thought exactly."

She gave one more exasperated sigh then tossed the keys back down. They bounced from her purse and slid under the cabinet. I reached down and retrieved them again, holding them to her face dangled on my fingertip. She laughed and snatched them back.

I let my hand slide up the back of her neck and pulled her face to mine. I kissed her slowly with purpose. Then, when I felt her body start to hint at a familiar rhythm, I punctuated with a small peck and stepped back.

"Wish me luck," I said. "Good luck."

"Bake me something good at the bakery today. We'll celebrate tonight."

I slipped on my heels, gathered up my bags, and looked back at her.

"Love you," I said as the door closed behind me.

I wish I had known that would be the last time I saw her.

3

"Congratulations, Ms. Zane!" Julie beamed from behind her desk in front of my office. She made sure to draw out the zzzzz in Ms. She didn't want to get reamed for accidently saying Mrs., like Mark Walker's assistant, Derek.

She stood tightly with her toes together, stretching up with her excitement. Or at least her feigned excitement. Her lavender skirt suit was neatly pressed, just as I required in case a client might interact with her. She coiled her dark hair onto her head and slathered a moderate application of makeup under her thin glasses.

I knew Julie gossiped with the other assistants about me. I knew she lamented my relentless demands and general cuntiness. However, if she had figured it out, she never advertised my lesbian disposition. I had no doubt she knew with Lei calling into the office, but she never asked. Without even my request, she kept it discreetly in my private life, and for that loyalty, I could forgive her healthy boss bashing.

"Thank you, Julie," I said as I walked past her into my office. I even let myself smile a little, genuinely.

Julie swooped up my messages and a couple of files from her desk before chasing me and gently closing the door behind her.

"Domestic Universe! Ms. Zane, this is huge!" Julie said.

She was teetering between her heels, absolutely vibrating. Her smile was so wide it was spreading down into the tendons of her neck. She was practically hugging her handfuls of folders and papers. Inside, I was jumping up and down like a prepubescent girl and smiling shamelessly like Julie, but I took a deep breath and kept my composure.

"I know, Julie. I know."

I couldn't resist reflecting a little bit of her joy and smiling back at her. Maybe she thought her elation would earn her more favor. Maybe she was ecstatic at the idea of where my coattails would take her. Maybe she even was genuinely happy for me. For once, motive did not matter to me. I was euphoric with success and could share that bliss with just about anyone at that moment.

"This is the biggest account the firm has ever landed," she reminded me as she placed the stack of messages in my palm. "They'll definitely make you partner this year."

I knew all this. All this was why this was the account. But it felt good to hear it again, out loud. I tried not to visibly bask in the sound of it.

Fuck it. I had made it. I could enjoy it just a little. I gently placed my hand on Julie's shoulder. "Thanks, Julie. You've been a great help through this."

Her jaw dropped open just a little before being pulled up into a coy smile. Apparently, I had succeeded in sounding sincere. She looked down and shuffled a bit, grinning to herself before she poised herself and snapped back into her role.

"Thank you, Ms. Zane." She hesitated briefly, seeming to take in the moment with a gentle grin on her lips. Then she caught herself. "Mrs. Johnston wants to see you."

"Excellent. Thanks again, Julie."

She smiled at me authentically one more time before she returned to her post outside my door.

"Shut the door behind you, please," I said.

As I heard the latch click, I closed my eyes and breathed out. I let my composure collapse momentarily as elation washed over me beneath my skin. I had done it; I had actually made it.

I melted into my high-backed chair and let my head rest against it. I could feel the smile stretching my cheeks. This degree of smile was reserved for Lei and unfathomable success. I opened my eyes and looked at my phone. My hand even twitched toward it.

I should call her, I thought. I should tell her right now. *I could tell her that I've made it, that I'm finally there. I'm in so deep that we can get married. Once I'm partner, I can get outed. I will have made them so much money and hooked so many fish that it won't matter. Domestic Universe nullifies any homophobic bullshit. We can settle down. I can ride this success and stop slitting throats to get here.* I let my fingers flirt with the receiver, imagining her blissful reception. Then reality sunk in. *She will just say she's heard this all before. She will just scoff in disbelief and frustration. She will suck the wind right out of my sails, deflate my excitement.*

It could wait until I got home, until I could convince her face to face.

"Rebecca?" I called as I gently knocked on Mrs. Johnston's open office door.

"Beatrix!" she replied from her massive desk consumed by teetering stacks of papers and files. "Come on in. Shut that door."

Rebecca commanded attention, regardless of her surroundings or company. She had the striking beauty of an aged child television commercial actress combined with the ferocity of a hungry business woman. She could not disguise her full breasts under her professionally appropriate tailored suits. She let her toned calves ripple strikingly from above her statement heels. Her blonde, styled locks fell recklessly down her back with never a hair out of place. Her soft and flawless features hardened clearly into resolve.

She was not one to be fucked with. She exploited her opposing qualities to her full advantage, strategically based on the situation. She was a ruthless role model. If she did not ignite my competitive need to succeed, I would have been wildly attracted to her.

I straightened my posture and lifted my chest to match her domineering presence and firmly closed her door behind me. The smile was still present on my lips but subdued from blind euphoria to confident victory. I would not let her see how much this win meant to me; this was just what I did.

"Have I ever told you that your name doesn't fit you?" she said, settling into her chair. She sat up rigidly straight and folded her hands calmly on the desk, amidst the war field of papers.

"More than once." I faked a friendly laugh. In my head, I rolled my eyes.

"Well, it doesn't. Feel like I'm addressing my great aunt or something. Anyway, I wanted to congratulate you personally on Domestic Universe. I'm sure I don't have to tell you what this means to the firm. And to your career. This is the account you needed to land partner and cement your future at this firm. Of course, nothing is official until year's end, but I can safely say you've guaranteed yourself."

"Thank you, Rebecca. I really appreciate all of that. I have been working toward partner for a long time."

"Yes, I know. You've made it."

Hold the smile inside. Temper your excitement.

Don't break eye contact. Maintain composure.

"What does this mean in the immediate?" I asked calmly.

"You'll manage the Domestic Universe account, obviously, as well as any accounts that come in as a direct result of it. When you transition to partner, we'll transfer several account managers under your direction. Then there is, of course, the pay raise, the stock options, and all the other perks associated with partnership. I'm sure you're familiar with all of these."

"Yes, of course. They've been a driving motivation."

"I figured. HR will go over all of the specifics with you when things become official."

"I understand."

"Good, good. For now, congratulations. Enjoy your victory. Celebrate. And keep up the good work."

"Thank you, Rebecca."

I stood slowly and extended my hand across her desk. She turned her head as she looked up at me and smiled out of one side of her mouth. Then she reached her hand to meet mine. Her skin felt smoother and warmer than I expected as it moved against my palm. I felt a slight tingle at the skin contact. I shook her hand firmly, then turned and stepped out of her office.

As I passed through the doorway, I dropped my stance just slightly, settling back into my own, more natural posture. I felt just a little bit of the pressure and pretense recede. I marched down the hall back toward my own office.

I had done it. I had made partner. After all those years of scratching and clawing, late nights, and Lei's tears, I was finally here. I could have floated down the gray little hallway. The light spilling in from the offices became ethereal; colors became brighter. I felt the sheer bliss of success lifting my chest. I was probably grinning like an idiot, drunk on myself.

Denise passed by me with a tight, forced smile. I caught myself in my euphoria and tugged myself back down into reality. I wiped the inebriated smirk off my mouth and tightened my face, raising a challenging eyebrow to her, establishing my dominance as usual.

"Congratulations, Beatrix," she muttered as she cast her eyes down.

Three years ago, Denise had tried to plant malicious seeds of rumors about me with our manager. She whispered in his ear repeatedly how I was fraternizing with another associate in the company, breaking the non-fraternization clause in our employment contract. The deepest insult in this was probably that this associate was a male douche bag.

I could have dispelled the rumor by coming out, but I would not give her the satisfaction of a scandal, of any potential advantage over me. I let her spin her bullshit and repaid her by fouling up her first major account and derailing her career.

She had managed to not get fired for the debacle but spent the following years in mediocrity. I looked down my nose at her as I watched her run bitch errands for associates that used to be her equals. I sneered to myself while she was relegated to copyediting. I raised my eyebrow to her any time she dared make eye contact to remind her of who she was fucking with.

I smirked to myself. Stupid bitch.

The smile was back on my face, dripping with condescension and satisfaction. I felt her turn to watch me as I passed her and put some extra stomp in my heels.

When my eyes focused ahead of me again, I saw Andrew making his way up the hall toward me. He didn't even bother to fake a smile or force out words. He gave me a sideways glare then rolled his eyes with a huff and stiffened his stride. I'm pretty sure I heard "bitch" in his breathing.

I had thrown him under the bus, let him think we were collaborating, then took the kill on the account. He was so young and green, so eager to work with me, trying to ride my coattails up the ranks. It was almost cute and endearing, but I could see the razors in his smile, sense the venom behind his empty compliments. When his nerves and inexperience tangled his tongue in the customer meeting, I stood up and eloquently owned the pitch we had developed. It got me a promotion; it was the first major step I needed.

This building was full of people I stepped on to get here. Today, it was all worth it.

I finished out my day in a haze. My mind continually circled back from storyboards and client calls and Domestic Universe contract review to Lei, to going home and telling her. She would make dinner, something homemade, complimented by something she had baked at work during the day. She always did, no matter how mad she was at me. I would play coy at first, making her extract the details from me, bit by bit, smiling and taking small bites of my food as I did it. She would puff out her bottom lip and pretend to stop talking to me. Then I would finally let her have it, calmly and smiling. She would believe me this time. She would be genuinely happy and tackle me amorously.

These fantasies infected my day until the light breaking my window began to fade. I smiled at the impending sunset, shut down my computer, and gathered my things. I took my time with anxious fingers, savored the excitement I felt welling in my chest. I let myself imagine a genuine smile breaking her face once more and felt my own cheeks turn up.

The office lights from the few still working spilled into the hallway, stretching out long over the flattened texture of thin, industrial carpet. I could still be working. I could always still be working, but tonight was hers. I took quick and measured steps until the hallway, the elevator, the lobby, and the large glass front doors passed over and behind me.

In the parking lot, I was alone, away from the prying, ever-watching, judging eyes inside the office. I walked from the building across the parking lot, feeling my posture relax in the minutest, feeling the tight mask of my features loosen. By degrees, with each stride further from the door, I felt my professional personification fade and fold into the back of my mind. I found my heels dancing and clicking across the pavement, singing a rhythm as I hurried home to tell her. Now, we could finally breathe and settle. We could be that couple she wanted.

The sun was retreating, leaving bloody streaks across the sky and clouds as the twilight muscled it below the horizon. I found a moment to look at it, a moment I never took any other night on my way home, a moment to appreciate the beauty in the way the day died, the way the sun finally submitted. I felt aware and undistracted in the attainment of my milestone. My eyes fully saw; my ears fully heard; my senses rose up to serve their base purposes. I actually saw the pine trees on the manicured medians, the nature forcibly juxtaposed in the lifeless glass and concrete. I breathed in deep and actually tasted the air.

Yet, at the edge of this foreign, relaxed freedom, I felt a bristle. Something on the peripheral of my perception irritated me, unnerved me. I let my eyes scrutinize the unmoving cars and the vacant asphalt; I let my ears prick to the edge of my hearing. There was nothing, yet my skin tightened at the primal call of something unidentified within me. It was the same sensation as that of feeling watched. I felt it not at the input of my senses but in the pit of my stomach, in my guts.

I did not have time to indulge wayward instincts. I told myself there was nothing there and brushed the apprehension coiling in my belly aside. My mind was overflowing with thoughts of what had passed in my day and what would pass in my night. Aside from a brief rapture in my surroundings, I did not exist in this present moment.

My keys were in my hand, poised between my fingers and pointed at the ready, not out of fear but out of anticipation. I was already in that car driving home; I was already walking into her welcoming arms. My vision tunneled, and that poignant sunset around me collapsed. I ignored the world at my senses and fell into that moment.

Then the world went black. The light swelled in my eyes then doused completely. I never heard You coming up behind me. I never had the chance to panic. I felt a tight embrace around my arms; I heard my keys hit the ground. My mind imploded on its own consciousness, tumbling into an abyss devoid of sight and sound. Before I could articulate what was happening to me, I was gone.

4

That leak was the first thing that finally roused me and introduced me to the headache splitting my skull and the bitter copper taste polluting my mouth. I woke up in that now familiar darkness with no idea where I was and no memory of how I got there. I opened my eyes to find my pupils and my mind reeling against a suffocating darkness.

My awareness lagged behind my consciousness.

Behind veiled eyelids, I had expected the soft light invading my bedroom; I had expected the gentle glow of the computer screen on my desk. I had expected some sort of familiar surroundings.

Instead, the air was cold and thin. By just taking a breath, I knew I was not home. The foreign air tasted like fear, and I felt the feeling rage up in me in kind. As panic raced over my skin, my body came to life.

I kicked out my legs—metals bars.

I flailed my arms—metal bars.

I struggled to stand—metal bars.

I could not fucking move. I could not fucking breathe. It happened so quickly. My mind was scarcely able to register my predicament before my instincts dissolved my brain. Thoughts started to break down as fear burned through every cell in my body. I was reduced to a thrashing, shrieking animal—an animal in a cage.

Once the animal within me ripped to the surface, cohesive thought disappeared. It was impossible to string together any semblance of an idea amidst the throbbing, screaming flood of fight and flight signals. My pulse undulated in the edge of my sight, giving the darkness sickening life, and causing me to hallucinate a chance of discerning anything out in the heavy black.

The darkness was potentially the most terrifying.

More than the acidic dread of claustrophobia permeating the muscles of my restricted limbs. I could feel my body, the metal bars. I could feel them, see what they were with my hands; I knew they were there. The darkness was an ominous mystery. More than anything, I did not want to know what was out there. I wanted to not be there.

It was all a blur, a blur of raging senses and blinding stimuli. It was a place my mind was incapable of comprehending.

I could not discern the memories of those first moments or hours even if I wanted to.

The connection between brain and body was impeded by biological imperative. Fight, flight, anything, everything in a desperate fury. It felt like nothing and everything simultaneously. My brain was awash with sensation and emotion, yet my mind was absent to interpret it.

I imagine You were waiting just outside that door, listening to me. A muddle of metal against flesh and rocking on concrete, a flurry of screams, moans, and cries. I can see You there, stoic and calmly awaiting my break. Like a parent waiting for the toddler to give up and finally realize all the kicking and screaming is futile. Maybe You were running a razor along a sharpening strap. Maybe You were rationing out my first meal. Preparing for something. You never wasted a second.

Fear and panic are just words. They in no way capture how I felt in those first hours in my cage. I could say them, scream them, carve them in my fucking arm a million times, and never fully express how the terror absolutely radiated from my bones. My mind abandoned me. It was not commanding my thrashing limbs or my throat screamed raw.

As the moments stretched over my flesh, the full rage of my initial reaction dissipated across the surface of my mind, fragmented into phases. I tried to block out the darkness, squeezed my eyes shut so the black at least made sense to my brain. It was too alarming to face with open eyes.

My body did not feel pain as I slammed it repeatedly and desperately into the bars, the shaking and shuttering echoing back at me. It felt only trapped. The energy and the fear built, swelled my muscles, exhausted my nerves at the simple denial of extension. I was disgusted at the sensation of my own legs coiled up against my belly. My arms felt like assailants so trapped against my torso. I hated my own flesh because I found it so imprisoned.

Yet, my physical resolve faded, crushed down by the darkness. My throat dried up and split after my voice continually tore through it. The adrenaline abandoned my cause and let pain and fatigue float up to my brain. I felt myself collapsing within and found what remained of my coherent mind at the bottom, buried somewhere beneath my failing primal self.

First, it was disbelief that formed chaos back into thoughts.

"This is not happening. This is not happening. This can't be happening. This can't be happening!" I whispered to myself over and over out of my harsh throat. I barely recognized my haggard voice so gripped by terror. I pulled my hair and kicked the bars futilely once more in hopes of rousing myself from this nightmare.

I dug around in my scrambled memories for some semblance of sense until the parking lot and those final light steps materialized from the haze. The day I was ripped from snapped back into my mind, and a greater wave of disbelief followed.

This just cannot be happening. I was just at work. I was just in the parking lot. I was on my way home to Lei. This was my fucking day!

Who would steal tonight from me? And why? What purpose could I serve in this fucking cage?

I cannot actually be in a fucking cage.

Does this shit even happen in real life? I felt the irrationality of a horror movie plot infecting my reality.

This simply could not be happening. I had no other explanation. Only that this could not be happening to me.

Then, almost instantly and seamlessly, rage consumed my chest. I rejected this fucking moment; I rejected this fucking situation. More than I did not believe it, I did not accept it. I would not accept it, not in body or mind.

I lashed blinding against my confinement, fueled now by anger instead of panic. I was bruising my feet, hands, arms, legs, but again, I could not feel it. I couldn't feel a fucking thing except sheer mania— some despairing blend of panic giving way to fury. Rage was only that same initial panic endowed with thought.

I ignored my feeble throat and released more pathetic screams.

"Help! HELP! HELP!"

As if anyone could hear me.

"Who are you? Why are you doing this to me? HELP!"

My words mocked me as they echoed back at me from the concrete. They made the room feel smaller, the walls feel thicker, the dark seem heavier. I hated the sound of my voice, the fear shaking in every syllable I screamed.

As if I had earned any answers. My words meant nothing anymore, to me or the world.

And in this void of reason, next came depersonalization.

I felt a gap expanding between the me that commanded from my mind and the me in the nerves of my flesh. The two separated, like stupid girls in the woods in a bad horror movie, both frantically running towards different failures to survive. The mental me began to calmly watch the frenzy of the physical me with detachment. The miscarriages of disbelief and rage created a rift within me.

I felt divided and compartmentalized, as if I could be of more than one mind, more than one person. Perhaps I ascended as a third party capable of viewing the conflict between the mental and the physical versions of myself. I watched the physical me contest a metal structure she did not even bend, and I watched the mental me attempt to reason an unintelligible circumstance. And somehow, for a brief instant, I felt divorced from it all. My consciousness tumbled through levels of myself, each reeling for some foothold in this darkness.

Yet all things eventually faded. Phases seized me then abandoned me. Passion diffused pain then discarded me back into its embrace. My mind whirled in desperation then collapsed exhausted. Thoughts began to roll lazily by in my omniscient third position above the storm, slow observation of my damning circumstances.

I am in a fucking cage.

I was taken. Someone took me.

Someone is keeping me here. For some awful reason. How am I ever going to get out here?

When are they going to kill me? They are going to kill me. Or worse.

When my instincts and my mind did unite and decide to chime in, it was with one singular contribution: *This is the end.*

And when all waves fell away, it was me and those bars at first. Those abrasive, cold, alien bars pressing into me at every angle, containing my fury. Fire burned down my limbs as they begged for freedom and mobility. My mind throbbed against my skull in sympathy. Every cell of my body felt simply trapped.

I tried to fidget to dispel the sensation. I attempted to shift my limbs around to deceive my body into feeling movement. My flesh was not so easily fooled. Perhaps because I could not banish the thought that I was confined in a tiny cage. The thought dripped through the cracks of my mind and pooled in my angry muscles, accelerated the burning denial in my body. I shook my legs and wrung my hands, taking ragged, forced breaths, trying to ignore the thoughts and the feelings.

Eventually, exhaustion snaked into my limbs. My muscles became slow and heavy, and I felt a weight descend on my forehead, pushing down even frightened thoughts. Pain seeped into the skin I kept slamming futilely against my cage. My fingers were gnarled stems of pain. I felt the swelling in my joints when I tried to shift them in my confined space. My toes were jammed into my foot from futile kicks; my knees burned in opened flesh.

Now, I found myself in defeat. My entire body throbbed from the fight that had accomplished nothing. I had not so much as bent a single slim bar; I had not so much as shifted the cage across the concrete. I was just as imprisoned—welted, bleeding, and now sobbing.

There were no tears. Maybe I didn't have any. My tongue was cleaved dry to the roof of my mouth, sealed to that horrendous coppery taste. My body just convulsed in a familiar pattern as the anguished sounds reverberated against the walls back at me. It was disgusting to hear these incoherent laments streaming from my own mouth, batted around the cold box. I sounded like a crazed animal; I could not even recognize my own voice amidst the shrieks and mumblings. I sounded less human by the moment.

The sounds grew weaker as the fire drained from me, as I reached the limit of both my body and mind. Defeat weighted me heavier than the physical exhaustion. A dense mind plunged me deeper far faster than any bodily drain. Then I slept, of all things. My cries calmed. I held still for the briefest moment, and the sheer, physical fatigue overwhelmed me.

The sleep began as black as my cell. Thick and paralytic. Then out of the dark, a swell of feverish dreams materialized upon the ruins of my mind, in a subconscious that could still pretend to be free. I dreamt of Lei, of course. The sunlight playing in her hair as dawn broke in through my window and fell on her tangled in my sheets. The torn jeans she was wearing when I met her and how just enough of her thigh was exposed to tease me. Those awful fucking woven hippie bracelets I bought for her.

Darkness greeted me when my consciousness did surface again. It was so obscure that it felt heavy on my eyes. They ached from scanning, searching, and stretching for light. When I closed my eyes, there was no difference; it was the same gaping void in front of me. It felt all the more hopeless.

My hands pulsated with the impressions of the crosses at the bars. I rubbed my fingertips over my palm, feeling the dents and the lines of pain. I rubbed them instinctually, trying to elicit the shape of my own hand. The joints in my hip and shoulder whined at so much constant and uncomfortable pressure. Weight and immobility packed into my bones, making them heavy with ache. There was only a thin blanket between me and the unforgiving base of the cage, which hovered unnervingly above the cold, concrete floor. My muscles felt thin and acidic. I just hurt, from my scalp to my toes, and I could not shift or move to alleviate any of it.

Lei remained entwined in the fleeting coherent thoughts in my head. How long had I been here? Surely long enough for her to miss me. Or would she just assume I was working late yet again? Breaking our plans as I always did. Maybe she thought I was out cheating on her, as if I had any time for that.

I imagined her without me for that first night. She would come home from work, the aroma of bread and pastries chasing behind her, thick enough to be a cloud. She would toss her keys on the counter, then her purse several steps later, breadcrumbs of her arrival like every night, things I would collect and consolidate by the door to the garage so she would be able to find them in the morning, things I would not be there to gather tonight. McAllister would be pawing at the back door, but it would take her littering junk mail all over the kitchen table before she let him in. She would smile beautifully, lighting up for him as he bounded around the house and jumped up against her.

She would wait for me, assuming I had to work late yet again, making herself a modest salad of only organic veggies and sip on her filtered water as she let

McAllister cuddle on the couch with her. She would half-watch cooking shows and wrinkle her nose when she paid attention until it got later and the night grew darker. She would text me then call me then curse me, convinced I was choosing my career again. Then she would huff and puff up and down the hall, slam through brushing her teeth and washing her face, and let McAllister take my side of the bed. Maybe she would curl up in the fetal position and let the sobs shake her body, just like I was here.

They would miss me. Lei would actually worry when she woke up in that bed alone with McAllister. She would call Julie first thing in the morning, questioning her of my whereabouts. Of course, I was working when Julie left. Julie would ask around the office, discern when I departed. They would be looking for me; they would be putting together the timeline.

Lei would surely call the police before the day was out. They would tell her she had to wait forty-eight hours. She would wait those forty-eight hours with growing fear. She would begin digging at her nails without thinking about it, until the cuticles began to bleed. She would be consumed by the thought, unable to focus on work, forgetting to feed McAllister.

Then the police would be looking. Maybe even by now. Weren't there security cameras in the parking lot? Couldn't that footage show my abduction? They would know what happened to me, and they would be looking for who did it. Perhaps tracking down a license plate, perhaps putting pictures on the news of a foolishly exposed face.

They would find me. Lei would not give up. She would stop sleeping until I was returned to her side. She would call the detectives assigned to my case so often they would roll their eyes at the sight of her number or message. She would never give up on me.

My vision of her faded to darkness. My hopes and all the things I told myself receded deep beneath the surface. And then it was just the darkness. Heavy, quiet, consuming. I fell in and out of sleep; I don't know how long or how many times. My dreams teased me; my nightmares mocked me. As time seemed to stretch out before and behind me, the line between the reality in my cage and the fog of my mind began to wobble.

Where the fuck am I? How will they find me here? Am I even in the same state? Am I even in a city or town? Am I even in a fucking house? What is in that looming darkness? At this point, only an unfathomable monster would match the fears brooding in my guts.

I wanted Lei. To my very core, amidst the turmoil of my mind, I only wanted to feel the softness in her touch. I cringed to imagine her gnawing and picking at her nails, worrying about me.

They are coming to save me.

They will never find me.

I am already dead, and this is Hell.

I could feel my sanity start to sidestep. So soon, if it even was soon. I was confined in my mind too long, lost in the seething wash of phases of captive grief and versions of my wilting selves. Time was rapidly becoming as forgotten a concept as light or movement. How long had I been here? I had not starved or thirsted to death; I had not pissed or shit myself.

A day? Two? Maybe three at the most?

Yet it already felt like a fucking eternity had passed in this black hole.

That drip, that fucking drip invaded my every thought, permeating my increasingly gnarled dreams. It filled the dark space around me and collided against my head. Over. And over. And over. And over.

It told me the room surrounding my cage was small. It told me I was somewhere wet and cold. It told me the floor was concrete and a good distance from the source of the drip. After a while, my mind started trying to convince me it sounded like a voice. I tried to hear Lei in the splash. I tried to feel McAllister's tongue in how wet it sounded.

I felt the confinement in every inch of my bones; an anxious, crawling claustrophobia that twitched and burst on my nerves. I wrapped my fingers through the bars, pressed the soles of my feet against them, and pushed until my muscles shook. The metal did not yield. I just wanted to stretch out; I just wanted to fucking stand up.

At this point, I would have cut off my own pinkie to do so. Followed by my whole hand or any body part to go home.

God, I wanted to stand up. I just wanted to fucking stand up! I felt the rage, the frustration, the burning panic welling up inside me again. I heard a guttural scream erupt from my core as I began to beat around the cage again. I howled wildly, shaking the bars, slamming my head against the cage.

What in the fuck was I doing?

I don't know what I expected to accomplish. I don't know that I was capable of thought in those frenzies. I pushed myself past my body's threshold, continuing to bash and bang even as the blood welled beneath my skin and my muscles trembled with weakness.

My body was completely dry; sweat crusted in a salty film on my skin. My stomach was a cavernous pit that had forgotten how to be hungry. Was I just going to be left in this hole to die? Was this how it was going to end, without so much as a glimpse of my captivity or captor?

Surely, if the point was just to erase me from the world, it would have already been done. The idea that I was taken for another purpose, yet unrevealed, was all the more worrisome.

I just had to stay alive until they found me. I just had to keep breathing until I inhaled air outside this box.

Maybe I just wanted to die here. If only I could forget Lei's face.

Her face was the one thing vivid on my mind. Her wide, dark eyes dominated her face, dwarfing her other soft features. They were like deep pools where sirens could dwell to entice me to her desires. Only her mouth could further seduce my attention, the way pale pink lines parted to reveal her front teeth that crossed ever so slightly.

Then, looking into my memories of her eyes in the dark, it became despair.

The sensations of my body began to fade and distort as the darkness in my own chest began to swell over my consciousness. It was a familiar sensation, an internal darkness I recalled in the muscle memory of my soul. The way suicidal tendencies crept up my spine after my first girlfriend shredded my heart. The way I wanted to crawl into the grave after my mother. It was like stepping into a warm bath; it was like lying down with an old lover; it was like a seductive gateway drug.

Perhaps if I curled up with this old friend, she would whisper sweet nothings in my ear to drown out that vile dripping. Maybe she would envelope me under her paralyzing blanket and keep me warm. She could drain me enough that I wouldn't feel all this pain.

"Lei…" I whispered. "Lei…"

I wanted my mind to go dark with her name on my lips.

Just as I really started to let go, I heard the door crack open.

5

The movement of the door was near deafening after so much silence. Just that steady drip. I forgot the drip the instant the door moved. The dim light spilling in from whatever lay on the other side of the door was glaring. I forgot the darkness as the light blasted in, filling and painting my cell, and slamming into my pupils. It was my first glimpse of my prison.

It was more damning than I had imagined from ,the sounds in the dark.

I felt my heart seize in my chest as adrenaline flooded my veins again. I curled up like an animal and crouched in the furthest corner of my tiny cage, huddling against those dreaded bars for safety now. I shielded my eyes against light that now blinded me and made my head ache.

I squinted until my sight adapted and the low light stopped assaulting my eyes. It took a moment for my mind to process the images transmitting from my retinas. Then, it started to process; I saw the dank, cold walls, my concrete box. *Holy fuck, I am in a closet or a basement somewhere?* I had no idea where. There was no indication. No window, no markings of any kind. Only the gray.

I cautiously let my gaze explore. I traced the walls slowly; then my breath stopped.

What in the fuck is on that wall? What is that?

Oh my God, is that a fucking whip? Is that rope? What are those straps? Dear Christ, so many blades.

I'm going to die in here. And it's going to hurt.

Then I found You. I laid eyes on my Master for the first time.

My heart stopped in my chest. Terrified does not begin to articulate it. My mind and my body locked up. I had no idea what to do, what to expect. My mind went inextricably blank, like I never knew how to think at all. I simply stared at You, slack-jawed.

You towered above my cage, a simply massive man. Your silhouette nearly consumed the doorframe, shielding me from the seemingly aggressive light. The first thing I noticed about You, amidst my terror, was how composed You were. It was striking enough to permeate my flailing mind.

You did not look like a psychopath, quite the opposite. My senses were heightened by fear, and I found myself inventorying every detail somewhere behind my physical panic. Your clothes, though basic, were clean, crisp, and fit You perfectly. Your posture was meticulously symmetrical, shoulders stacked over hips stacked over knees stacked over ankles. You had Your gloved hands interlaced as You looked down and observed me in kind.

There was no expression on Your face. No anger, no hate, no excitement, no glee. It was simply blank and slack. Your face was clean, as if hair did not even grow there to be shaved. Your dark hair was cut short and shaped tightly against Your head, every hair in place.

Your eyes were large and took me in whole, and Your facial features were strong. A nose that could cast its own shadow, cheekbones that jutted out harshly, a strong jaw. Everything about You would be striking in a normal setting, much less cowering below You in a metal cage.

You stood there for the longest moment. You set both feet inside my world and remained just inside the doorframe, parallel to it, in a perfect formation. I was frozen, waiting for You to move, waiting for You to speak, waiting for any indication of what I was in for. You appeared as much of a mystery as the darkness itself.

But You were a man, so my immediate thought was simple. *He's going to rape me.* Of course, You were going to rape me. That is what men kept women captive for. I waited in anguish to hear Your zipper drop, to feel You drag me from my cage and pin me down. I cringed at just the thoughts. I think You were amused at my flinching and my fear, tickled by how naïve I could be.

When You did move at last, Your footsteps were slow, methodical. You waited, watched my every reaction. In a calm and measured stance, You drank me in. I would say You were savoring my raw state, relishing our beginning. I tried to look up and meet Your face, learn my captor; however, the fear kept slapping my head back down. My instincts demanded I keep all parts of me close and tucked in.

Without a word from You, that moment passed, and my education began.

As You approached the cage, I screamed at You. I attempted to raise my hackles and scare You off.

"Get the fuck away from me!"

"Who are you?"

"What the fuck do you want from me?"

You slowly opened the cage door, and I felt my heart slamming against my ribs. Then Your hand stretched in toward me.

"Let me go!"

"Don't touch me!"

"No! NO!"

"Fuck you!"

I puffed my chest, hardened my body language, blinked back tears of sheer fear. You effortlessly snatched a flailing ankle out of the air with a gloved hand and dragged me from the cage and out onto the concrete floor in one fluid motion.

I felt my limbs bounce harshly along the bars and the opening to the cage. All my floundering grasps were entirely futile. I only felt the bars slip past my twitching fingers. The floor greeted me harshly, my skin audibly slapping against it and the air forced out of my lungs. I lay stunned and breathless for a split second before recoiling from You again.

I scrambled, tucking all my limbs into my body, huddling down as low and as far away from You as possible. As I wrapped my arms tightly around myself, I noticed that I was no longer wearing my tailored button up and suit. The cloth that greeted my fingers was thin and baggy. Where had these clothes come from? When had I been changed?

I did not dare look up. I did not dare see what was coming for me. I only trembled, waiting to learn my purpose in this prison. I heard You step away from me, in the direction of that terrifying wall; I heard Your fingers at work selecting an implement. Yet I continued to keep my eyes down on these foreign clothes draped over my body.

I felt Your footsteps come up behind me. I tightened into my fetal ball. You slowly reached down and guided the hem of my shirt up to expose my back. My heart and my breathing stopped. I was quivering uncontrollably.

Then that first introduction of pain. The strap. I felt the thick, supple leather paint a sting across my back, tearing the pain deep into my flesh. The sensation blanked out the world; my mind only knew the shape of the lash, the pattern in which my nerves ignited.

At such exquisite pain, I could not resist glancing up. I could not control my curiosity, my blatant need to visualize my attacker and attack. You kept as much distance between us as You could. You stood above me, cold and stoic, and let the strap lick Your commands over my flesh.

I saw Your shape, tall and clean, in black. Black clothing, black hair. Perhaps I even saw black eyes. I could only manage to steal a glimpse of Your figure before the strikes bore my head down again.

Do as you're told.
Shut your mouth.
Respect my control.
Forget that old life and old self.
You are mine.

Each command split my flesh; each instruction bit and drew blood like a vampire. It would take weeks before I understood the language of the lash.

How I howled at You. Something changed in me when You parted my skin for the first time and invited the warm blood out into the dusty air. An electric rush of adrenaline blazed through me, and I suddenly lunged at You wildly. The animal was surfacing. I leapt as a blur of clawing limbs. I imagine it was a very pathetic attempt, but I was led only by instinct.

You greeted me with that strap around my neck. You managed to loop it around my neck effortlessly amidst my thrashing arms. I felt the pressure against my neck, the constriction of blood and air, and my fight diffused.

My sight instantly clouded as You denied my lungs air, reprimanding me until the world was fuzzy enough to dull the pain. My defiance was choked into feeble gasps.

In the haze of oxygen deprivation, my mind retreated back from my flesh. Even when You released the strap and returned to the lashes, it became just a distorted cloud. I remember the ever- throbbing pain migrating around my body, stopping to pay attention to each new lash. I remember the taste of the concrete when You released my throat and let me suck air off the floor again.

I remember thinking, *I am here to suffer.*

After it was over, I lay twitching and whimpering, curled up in a pathetic, welted, and bloody ball on the floor. You stood over me immobile for an instant—a perfectly silent and paralyzed moment that stretched out into each second, so thick I could feel time slow down through my pain. Caught up in the intensity of the stillness, I had stopped breathing again.

As You took a step, I heard Your shoe scrape across the concrete, reanimating the scene. I let a breath puff against the floor and back into my face, and my chest began to rise and fall again. I left my skull heavily draped, staring down at the floor, as I heard You move. I listened to the strap gently graze the wall as You hung it in its place. Your steps neared me again; Your shadow fell over me as You crouched. I felt a gloved hand rest on my shoulder, and I flinched desperately.

Slowly, calmly, You simply pushed my shoulder and rolled me onto my back. I felt the pain light up in the straight lines of the lash as my wounds met the cement. I squinted and prepared myself for more punishment. Yet none came. The lesson was over. Your face was no longer stern and vacant; the hard edges had relaxed.

I flinched as You crouched down to me, as if I could curl any tighter into myself. You waited, frozen in a composed squat, until my twitching subsided. Then I felt Your gloved hands guide me to a seated position. At some point, I had started crying, and my sobs trembled my body as I sat hunched over.

I did not know what to expect.

I did not know what to hope for.

You carefully cleaned the wounds of the shell that remained of me. Your harsh abuse had given way to a soft touch as You pressed a cold cloth to my welts and wiped away the blood. Then You gently guided me and placed me into the cage, like a seed into the ground.

With the lock to my cage secured, You departed for a moment, leaving the door to my cell ajar. I wished I had the strength to chase Your path and try to catch a glimpse outside this box, but my body was too depleted from the pain and the fight. I could only lie crumbled at the bottom of that cage.

I did not even strive to look up when You returned. I let myself stare through watery eyes at the blank wall while You still granted me light to see it. I heard You unlatch the lock and open my door. I felt You place something near my feet—what I later would fumble through the darkness to discover as adequate food and water. Enough to buy me another day inside this cage.

I knew You were gone when the darkness fell around me again. Despite my hunger and thirst, I did not move to the provisions at my feet. I let myself wallow in the hum of my pain as Your lesson secretly began to permeate my mind.

The beating left me in shock, rattled everything in my head much deeper than my dark and unexplained imprisonment. I did not know the woman You pulled out of the cage, who crumpled into a protective ball so quickly. I had not made the decision to give up, to lay there and cry as You cleaned my wounds. Fear, survival, abject confusion had made me a stranger. Even more than the hum of pain on my nerves, I felt the crushing fear at the foreign feeling of myself.

When I think back on this night, our first night, I can barely stand to remember that old foolish me who met You, with my oh-so-progressive and liberal lesbian relationship and my oh-so-important high-powered career. How I stupidly resisted You. I was so ignorant, so blind as I clung to the idea of freedom, to the belief that I couldn't be owned.

He is a nut case. He just has to be some fucking nut case, I told myself in the painful dark. *Something is broken is his head. Clearly, it has to be. What kind of demented piece of shit keeps a woman in a cage? What kind of loser just takes someone to beat them? He is just fucked, and I am just a casualty.* I repeated to myself over and over, *I will get out of this; I will find a way out and back to her.* I told myself there was a way back to that precious life.

Why did I fight so long? What did I expect to gain by resisting so hard? Could I honestly believe there was ever any hope? I convinced myself for a while, but I think that deep down, in the depths of my heart, I knew from that first moment. When my mind said it was the end, it meant it was the end of the me I knew, the end of that life.

Yet eventually, it faded. Even that first night. The adrenaline died out. My muscles burned and quivered. The first wave of hope died faster than I expected, faster than it had when I wrestled alone. As the anger and fight drained out of me, dripping from my body as if I was bleeding out, I wrapped up in despair. Sadness cradled me against those bars so uncomfortably pressing into my hips, my sides, my shoulders. The tears burned hot down my cheeks as I just whimpered to myself.

My mind crumpled down to its one vestige of clarity—Lei. I imagined those wide, dark eyes greeting me at the door when I returned home from work. I imagined my news transforming her irritation into bliss.

"I made it," I whispered to her between sobs. "We can finally have it all."

6

After that first lesson, You left me to process alone. Pain was radiating over me. I could articulate the pattern of welts in my mind from how my nerves sang out in chorus. Long stripes horizontally across the widest part of my back. The lines mingled at their root then splayed out at wide angles. I imagined the welts I could not see or reach to touch. My skin was humming so hard, I practically vibrated against the bars as I lay lifeless in the fetal position. Warm tears would have steadily poured down my cheeks, but my body did not have fluids to waste like that.

My biological needs rose to rival the sensations of my injuries. I finally hobbled and crawled to turn around in my cage. The square was impossibly small. Just turning around was an endeavor, especially on my fatigued and injured body. I had to move slowly, by degrees, before I was able to fumble through the darkness to discern what You had left me. My fingers clumsily articulated a small bottle of warm water and a couple of crusts of bread. They felt foreign in my hands; my fingers began trembling in anticipation.

Awkwardly, I tried to eat and drink hunched down on my hands and knees, craning my neck upward, feeling the pressure bloom in my contorted shoulders and neck. There was nothing natural about feeding in this condition, just as there was nothing natural about being locked in a cage in a concrete box in the dark.

I had not realized I was still sobbing until I went to lift the bottle to my lips. It quivered and splashed against my mouth. I stopped and breathed deliberately to calm myself. When my sobs subsided, I gulped desperately at the water. My mouth rejoiced at the fluid; I could not drink it fast enough. Long before my thirst was quenched, I heard the bottle crumple empty.

I snatched up the bread and inhaled it, barely chewing the substance before swallowing it down. The bread sucked the freshly introduced moisture back out of my mouth. The introduction of food after so many hours set my stomach ablaze. The full bottle of water did not even wet my throat. I should not have ingested so gluttonously; I should have known, even this early, to ration.

With an empty plate and an empty bottle, I simply and sadly dropped my head, curling up on the small blanket. With my writhing stomach muffled, I thought of Lei again. No matter what happened, I could not stop thinking of her. She was the disease of my heart. Loving her so much made this box all the more painful. Remembering her, longing for her was the real torture. I wanted to die every time I envisioned the curve of her hip or felt the warmth of her skin.

She began to mock me from outside this cell. Even if she did gnaw off her fingers with fear for me, she sat free in the comfort of our home. She was able to stand

and walk and pace. Why had she not found me with all that freedom yet?

Why was I here long enough to feel the sting of Your wrath?

My own thoughts were turning to poison as my stomach curled around the meager crumbs and swallows. I had no refuge if I soured the thoughts of Lei. I chose to blank out my mind. I curled up with my bodily pain and focused on the sound of my own breathing over that never-ending drip.

How long did You leave me alone to break me? Cut off from all interaction. Sealed in my dark little box until You could starve out my pride and delusions of self, carve me down to just a shell. It felt like days, but everything felt like days and years in the darkness. I could count the seconds, but the numbers began to grow too massive for me to keep my grip. They too faded away into the black. I just knew it all felt like a horrific eternity.

I knew it could not have been too long. I still had not died for lack of food and water. My body still had not processed my tiny meal enough to force me to soil myself. Dark hours were ambiguous and shapeless.

Then out of the darkness, with no real pattern or indication, You returned, just as unexpected as the first time. My heart slammed into my chest and pulled me back into a sloppy consciousness at the sound of the door. My muscles tensed in unison and brought me slamming up too rigidly for my space. The bars halted my ascent with a sting deep in my hair. I ignored the sensation and recoiled deeper into myself.

You looked exactly the same, the same pristine plain clothes, the same gloves. Fear gripped me tighter than before, specific, channeled fear at knowing what was coming. The tension wound around my chest, clenching my heart into struggling beats that knocked against my ribs. I did not waste time trying to think, trying to forecast my pain. I only thudded with my pulse as I waited.

Your shape meditated briefly in the space before moving to the lock of my cage. Again, You denied me so much as a glance. With Your intimidating gaze downcast, I took the opportunity to actually look hard, to do more than glance and observe my captor. Time appeared to freeze to grant me the chance.

You did not look as I would have imagined a sadistic kidnapper. In my darkest nightmares of abduction, You were never the figure appearing from the shadows. You did not have wild and crazed eyes. You were not unkempt at the distraction of mental illness. You looked like any man. Clean cut in a suit in an office like mine. Capped by a baseball hat coaching little league from the sidelines. Smiling drinking a beer at a bar. You looked alarmingly normal.

You did not meet the measure of a monster forged in my head.

As the bars parted, my body was vibrating in a blurred and twisting dance of anticipation and terror. *Is it going to be another beating?* My very skin trembled at the thought. *Is he going to rape me?* My vagina itself clenched against the idea. Is he going to kill me? My heart hesitated in a beat to both dread and hope. These would become familiar and stupid questions from a naïve and imperceptive mind.

Your gloved hand broke into my space. The intimacy I had unfortunately formed with these bars made the square of my cage feel like part of my body, the bars like additional bones. Your intruding limb felt like a violation, causing my face to wrinkle, drawing my lip up toward my nose as my limbs pulled closer to my body. I flinched but also felt myself rising, leaning toward You. Did I want to hide in this cage, or did I want You to pull me from it? It seemed like an eternity with Your fingers hovering in front of me.

Your grip on my wrist was so stiff and impersonal.

I could feel the sticky texture of the thin leather of the gloves. I imagined the fingertips, the skin beneath the gentle pillow of cow flesh. I wanted it to be skin, even Your skin that I so vividly feared. Anything but cold concrete and metal.

It was a primal desire to feel something natural. The way I vaguely remember craving the warmth of my mother's embrace, the softness in her palm as it cradled my cheek. The materials containing me were all dead and made me feel all the more removed and deprived. There was no comfort in such hard surfaces; there were only additional sources of pain.

You tugged me firmly, with resolve. For a split second, my instincts defied, and I leaned back. My muscles tightened instinctually, pulling me away from You. I felt Your grip tighten, calling me back to myself. My cells remembered bumping along the cage and being scraped against the concrete. It was foolish to resist You. I clenched my teeth and forced my resistance aside. I made the deep physical resolve to release, to simply submit in this moment. I cowered and just followed the direction. I ducked my head and crawled out from my cage, keeping myself close to the floor, keeping a safer distance from You.

My entire body was trembling. I wanted to look up at You, but my muscle memory was only that of our previous meeting. I could feel the lashes; I could taste the blood. So I hunched, and I waited.

You still did not look at me. You released me to hover at Your feet and tugged the lonely string on the light bulb. I didn't even know there was a light bulb. Had it been on last time? I hadn't even taken the time to notice; I was far too distracted.

With eyes not blurred by panic, I finally saw my prison. I took the time to face more than just the cement box. The walls were hard and blank, broken only by the meticulous hanging of all Your tools. I could not look upon them long without that body- shaking fear rising in me again.

I chased the sound and found that incessant drip.

It was nothing more than droplets sneaking through the ceiling and pooling far below on the equally gray floor.

It was all so much smaller in the light.

You moved and pulled a bucket out from the corner behind the door. I had never made it out in the dark; it had been a silent intruder lurking out of sight. You set it at the edge of the light and stepped aside. I could tell You wanted me to do something with the bucket, but what the fuck was I supposed to do with this bucket? I stood dumbfounded for a moment, wanting to look into Your face for answers but only staring sheepishly at the floor. I could feel Your posture stiffen; I could sense Your impatience and displeasure infiltrate the air. My heart was beating faster, harder, but I still did not know what You wanted from me.

Finally, You stepped forward. I immediately dropped lower and raised my arms protectively.

What is he going to do with a bucket? What in the fuck will he do with that bucket?

You reached down, and I felt Your gloved fingers wrap around my shoulders. There was no tension, no firmness in the grip, which was all the more unnerving. It was only guidance as You pulled me to standing and moved me to the bucket.

I shifted at first, wanting to fight You, yet I caught my disobedience quicker this time and dropped the rigidity from my muscles. I forced compliance through my veins, as bitter a taste as it left on my tongue. Your touch was gentle; what could You mean by this bucket?

You took my shoulders again and turned me away from the bucket. Then You reached down and tugged my pants and underwear to my ankles. I felt a shockwave slam through my bones at the exposure, as the dank concrete air licked my bare flesh. My hands dropped automatically, futilely attempting to cradle myself back to modesty. My heart began to race again, heightening me to another level of fear.

RAPE! RAPE! RAPE! The alarms blazed in my brain.

I wrapped my arms around myself and wanted to die. The fear of Your next impending touch fell as a sickening weight in my stomach. As if thin layers of cloth had been protecting me until now. My body, my privacy was torn down with those meager clothes. Everything that had belonged to Lei, every part of my physical body that I had given to her lay bare and displayed, taken from me. I felt hot and shameful tears starting to wet my cheeks. There was no anger in this violation, no rage against this stripping. I only felt myself shrinking into despair.

I waited for the next, more traumatic step as I felt anxiety bubble into the back of my throat tasting like vomit. However, You simply stepped back and waited, crossing Your arms and looking expectantly.

Why is he stepping back? Why isn't he touching me, assaulting me? What was the point of stripping me from the waist to leave me standing here?

Yet the distance between us calmed my fright, somehow made me feel less naked and vulnerable. My space was mine, even if nothing else was. Confusion swelled in its place. Then You turned Your back to me and spared me even Your watchful eyes.

What does he want me to do? He wants me to do something with this bucket. What could he want me to do with this bucket?

I felt my bladder swelling against my pelvis in the still moment. My bowels clenched as if my body knew what my mind could not discern. The epiphany began to glimmer; the bucket was my toilet. I shifted uncomfortably, bound at the ankles by my own panties. It had been so long; I had forgotten that I did have to go.

Humiliated, I stared down at the concrete and squatted shakily while You stood stoic and uninterested with Your blank back to me.

7

I ran my hand over the landscape of the meager blanket, searching out the plate. My pupils were completely blind plunged back into the darkness, but I gradually noticed You had left the light on the other side of the door on. It was just enough for my eyes to slowly dilate and stretch.

I heard the crinkle of the plastic water bottle against my fingertip then turned my other hand out until it grazed the curve of the plate. Keeping my hands as markers against my food, I pulled myself from being hunched at the back of the cage and crouched forward over the plate, like a hungry animal, looking back and forth for things I couldn't see, things that weren't there.

I learned this time. I took one stingy sip from the bottle before forcing myself to close it again, even as my parched throat wilted and begged for more hydration. The water swelled slick and warm on my tongue. I felt my very cells rejoice in the sensation. Then they began screaming when I pulled the bottle back from my mouth.

My lips were quivering, but I held to the resolve I knew I needed. Ration.

My eyes had finally adapted enough to give the terrain of the plate shape. I cautiously poked the puddle of paste at its center. It was cool and chunky. My stomach would have turned in other circumstances, yet I put my finger to my mouth and tasted the glob on the tip. My taste buds were peaked. I could have tasted the metal of the plate itself. Salty, thick. Some kind of beans maybe? My stomach didn't care; it sang out. This was more food than my previous plate. Had I behaved?

I slopped some of the beans onto one hunk of bread. The crust was rough against my fingertips even as the paste dripped over it. I took a breath and compelled myself to eat slowly.

Control was excruciating. Every primal part of me gave no shit for the logic in pacing myself, just as it denied the necessity of bowing to my captor. Yet I had to keep a shred of my mind. I told myself it was the brain that survived, not the beast.

I placed the tempting remains beside the water bottle and curled up on my side.

I closed my eyes to shut out the darkness. Lei still danced through my brain. The way she walked on her toes when she was barefoot, betraying her childhood served in ballet. The way she was perpetually covered in flour from the bakery, how it created a paste beneath her fingernails and behind her ears even after she showered. The way she used McAllister as a body pillow, curled up against his back when she went to bed without me.

These thoughts left my body feeling empty and vacant. Forgotten. My flesh was lonely in a way I did not know how to bear. The emotional cut drawn in their void was far more vivid than the physical torments You had administered. I could only desperately try to escape into what was left of my mind.

"I missed you today," she said into my hair. I could hear her fingertips moving over my scalp as they entwined in the short strands. I could feel her skin radiating soft warmth against mine. My nerves tingled and raised up in my skin to meet her; they craved her even when she was here in my arms. I closed my eyes so I could only feel her, read her in the language of her touch. She felt perfect; that was the word branded in my brain from the first time my fingertips brushed her flesh. Perfect. As if my body knew her already, had been missing her all this time. I wrapped both arms around her and clutched her close, inhaling deeply, trying to breathe her in. I could feel, when I held her like this, that she forgot all my bullshit and understood what my body was saying.

I reached out in my dream, stretching out for her.

My hand bumped into the cold bars, rejected. They felt more lifeless and frigid than ever. I felt more alone. If that was possible.

Why have they not found me? How has she not dug me out of this hole yet? How can she leave me here like this?

Even in her deepest, most torturous worry for me, she was free to stand, to seek comfort. She was free to live. I felt resentment blossom in my chest, leaving trails of jealously along my heart. I was forsaken here by anyone and everyone in my life.

The thought crossed my mind like a shadow. I wished You were here in this cell with me. Once the desperate thought registered, nausea instantly seized my stomach. The alien idea invading my brain surprised me and caused me to gag instantaneously. I heaved without conviction and fell instead to confused, open-mouthed sobs.

How could that thought be in my head?

How could I even think that?

How could I want You, the very person who did this to me?

Did my pathetic desperation know no bounds?

It felt like another person was inside my brain, poisoning my thoughts, polluting who I was. There was an intruder blossoming inside me, obscured by the multiple turning versions of myself. You planted this betrayal in my flesh with the lash. You did this to me, as well. Yet I felt it resonate at my core.

And that terrified me.

I felt the tears rising again, burning behind my eyes and across my whole sinuses. Tears for the cold, empty space beside and around me. Tears for the stranger blooming inside me—Your design gradually starting to take shape inside the gray matter in my head.

I granted myself another restricted sip of water to match the tears I was losing; then I closed my eyes and tried to shove myself into sleep.

Any escape would work.

8

The bucket changed me. Some part of the civilized or independent or human me died wavering over that plastic cylinder. Some part of me couldn't endure the embarrassment.

The humiliation.

The depersonalization. The dehumanization.

I had been pissing and shitting on my own in normal toilets, some more civilized than others, since I was a fucking child. Since I was toddling around and struggling with English. It was part of what defined me as a functioning person; it was part of my right as a member of society. It was something that was mine.

This violation was different than being ripped from my heels and my life. It was different than being confined in my miserable cage inside my dismal and dark cell. It was different than the savagely executed beating.

It was a primal blow, and it planted the seed of my hatred.

Hatred for You bloomed deep in my chest. It stirred her back from under and behind my fear. The bitch that clawed her way to partnership in five years, the cunt who once attacked a biker in a bar for calling her a dyke. What was I doing cowering to You? What was I doing missing You? You were the impediment between me and Lei; You were the saboteur of my arrival at the promised land.

You were my captor. You were a psychopath.

How could I have been so weak to waiver so quickly and so easily? One little beating and I was groveling like a pussy. A few days in the dark and I was already longing for Your wretched company.

What. The. Fuck.

My next thought was simple, focused: I had to escape. Clearly, no one was coming for me; I had to get myself out.

But when? How? I convinced myself that I just needed to wait for my opportunity. I fooled myself into thinking You would grant me such a window. At this point, I appreciated that You were not a smash- and-grab psycho, that You had some sort of more intelligent design at work. However, my mind had not even begun to scratch the surface of Your depth.

Day after day, You moved through my room with abbreviated appearances of Your icy presence, only slipping food inside my cage, only changing out my bucket, denying me even eye contact. Hour after hour being trapped with my rampant thoughts deafening.

I didn't need Your attention. I would not be in here long.

The panic seized and abandoned me in waves, twirling and dancing with a startling apathy. I scoured my memories. I was walking to my car. Just walking to my car like every other night.

The parking lot was empty, wasn't it?

Just dormant cars, weren't there?

I dove with both hands into that moment, scratching the nails of my mind down the asphalt trying to grip it. I squinted my eyes shut hard, closed out and ignored my ears until I smelled the twilight on that night. I stood apart, watching myself move through the parking lot.

Rebecca's sleek silver sports car lounged in the coveted first spot; often there before I arrived, frequently there as I departed under the streetlights. That car always stole my attention, but there were others. Nameless, faceless vehicles just creating the scene.

I could not pull details from a focus I never had. I could not scan things I never saw. I only remembered the sun dying in the sky. My eyes were detached, lost in thoughts of Lei, basking in my bullshit success. The memory had a haze around it different than degeneration or intoxication; it was trying to remember something I never experienced at the time in the first place.

I reviewed waking up in the darkness, that first wave of terror shaking me to my core, rattling my bones deep within their soft flesh, my mind blanking before abandoning me to my primal instincts. Fear began to rise in me again just flirting with the thought.

I am a fucking kidnapping victim. I am in a fucking cage in someone's fucking closet.

And I am going to fucking die in here.

The overwhelming surreal quality of this reality, the captivity, had my mind reeling, groping at the surface like someone dragged under a wave. I came up for air in the strangest flashes of my rapidly fracturing mind.

I woke up to my soft bed enveloping me. I opened my eyes to see Lei's sleeping face, mouth hanging slightly open. I heard her soft snores pluming against my face as the daylight invaded our space. I smiled to myself at the warmth, at the comfort. Then I stretched as

I eased out of bed. I stumbled, still half dozing, across the room and opened the bathroom door.

And walked into my cell. The cold concrete greeted my feet, jarring and harsh. I felt the chill climb my throbbing skin and sore muscles, making me curl tighter into myself. I felt that constant, nagging, guttural fear lapping at the base of my brain. It began to crush me again, and I collapsed to my knees, dropping my face into my hands so I could feel my tears.

And I felt a warm hand, soft and heavy, rest on my shaking shoulder. I snapped my head up to make out my mother's shape beside my small bed. My Rainbow Bright comforter was wound tightly in my tiny fists. Her hand swept over my hand and down through my hair. *Just a nightmare, my baby. I'm here. I'm right here. I got you.* I reached out to touch her face.

And my fingers bumped into the metal bars.

I always resurfaced in my cage, in my room, in Your possession. As the lonely days began to blend together and my floundering mind swallowed the world, I throbbed for human interaction. Anything more than Your momentary appearances in this place. First, I ached for her. I imagined the feeling of her warm skin, the way it lit my own on pleasant fire, the way she circled her fingers around my shoulder blades as I held her. Then I tumbled farther back, longing for my mother's warm embrace, the way she would envelope my child body, the way her body heat would just cradle me. I even lamented not having McAllister's stinking breath pluming into my face. I missed them all. In every cell of my cold and starving body.

Lei was plaguing my every thought, pounding harder and harder in my brain by the hours ticked off by the drip. Her smell, that warm aroma of rising dough and sugar, snaked through the cold air around me. I felt her fingers swirl and grip the back of my neck the way she did when she kissed me with purpose. I heard the awkward way she stifled her roaring laugh in front of people she didn't know well echoing at me from the concrete.

She was like a ghost haunting the walls of my cell. An impatient ghost. I had to get out of here, had to get back to her. She was calling to me in these excruciating memories. She beckoned me from where I knew she was curled up around McAllister on the couch, wet tears on her cheeks, sobbing into his fur. Missing me.

They weren't going to find me. It had been too long now; I could feel it. Hadn't I heard somewhere that if they don't find the missing in the first forty- eight hours, they don't find them alive? Or at all. Wasn't there a show about that? I could not wait here for my saviors to burst through the door to my cell, guns drawn and EMTs behind. There would be no rescue; I had to get myself out of here. I forced my thoughts to turn out of the wayward panic and circle back to escape.

Escape had to be the hope in this dark.

The light would blind me at first, so intense after all the darkness. I would stumble and squint as I shielded my eyes, but I would keep running. I would burst out of this hole in the ground, this dungeon in a basement, this shed in the woods. My legs would burn with atrophy, and my lungs would heave unpracticed, but I would not stop running. Even as the ground tore open my bare feet, I wouldn't feel it.

I would only feel the freedom and the outside air on my face.

There would be a torrent of police and doctors and officials, and the still center of that spinning world would be Lei. She would emerge unmoved and unchanged from the chaos. Her eyes would be red from so many nights spent weeping, but the fresh tears welling in her eyes would be joy, relief.

I would hobble to her on my broken body. I wouldn't see anyone else but her. And when I felt her arms encircle me, when I felt her heat radiate against me as we embraced, I would know it was over.

I thought of the reunion more than I dwelled on my plans, yet I spent the next few days plotting my escape. I never could have conceived how deeply laid Your plans truly were. I would pick the lock on the cage. I would lift something sharp off of You and school myself in lock picking. I would crouch in wait for the opportune moment. I would bludgeon You with the metal plate from my last meal, somehow enough to disorient You. I would run and run. I would find help. I would return to her.

Idiocracy like that is for the movies. My dominos were never to line up so neatly.

It is embarrassing to remember how sloppy I was at first. Like that first night, just lunging at You like an animal, hoping to knock You aside long enough just to run. You barely moved when I collided with You, just rocked back onto Your heels and stared down at me, blank or maybe faintly amused. You simply locked a hand around my wrist as I wildly scrambled for the door, slowly contorted me down to my knees where I belonged. I must have looked so stupid. It was a wonder You didn't give up on me and just bury me as a failure then.

Once the seed began to blossom in my brain, I spent a day or two scouring my options. You did not leave me much to work with. The only tool I could identify was the fork You began including with my food when I was elevated past the unidentified paste. The fork would have to be my key; it was all I had.

I actually tried to pick the cage lock with a bent fork, like some lame caper movie. In the dark, I curled my fingers around the edge prong and pushed and pulled until the metal dug into my skin. My hands trembled at the exertion, and my breath squeezed out from pursed lips until the metal yielded. I brought the prong away from its siblings then curled myself up against the door of my cage.

I sat awkward and hunched against the bars, the steel digging into my hip and shoulder. I could only fit my hands out of the spaces between the thin bars and only to the wrists. With both hands shoved out of different slots, wrists pressed to the point of wavering sensation, I juggled the fork between my fingers, trying to maneuver it in the direction of the lock.

The metal spun from my fingertips and softly clanged on the floor. And my heart sank with it.

Thankfully, it tumbled close to the cage. I moved my hands to the lowest slots and scraped my nails along the concrete. I could not see the fork; I could only hear it shift on the floor when I grazed the cold metal. I reached until my tendons whined and managed to dig the fork close enough to grip. I manipulated the fork and my hands back through the bars, then back up to the lock and out again.

This time, I managed to point the bent prong at the lock and fumble it against it. As if I knew anything about locks or spindles or whatever the fuck was inside them. I jabbed it clumsily at the lock like an anxious schoolboy. The tip managed to penetrate, but it was too thick to be effective.

The fork fell again, as did my hope. As if You would give me a utensil that I could manipulate into freedom in any imaginable scenario.

I retrieved it once more only to cover my attempt. I grunted until I bent the prong back, hopefully unnoticeably straight again. Then, in the dark, I ran my fingers over the metal repeatedly until I convinced myself it was restored to an original and unsuspecting condition.

The morning after the unsuccessful fork debacle, You lifted the lock in Your hand and hesitated. You turned it in the dim light just a bit, to ignite the scratches. My heart completely stopped, and I heard the void of my pulse in my ears. I could feel my eyes spreading wider and wider.

You smirked out of the corner of Your mouth and just resumed Your task as planned. I remained frozen in panic as Your hand entered. I did not know what to do. *What is he going to do to me? Is he reaching in to snatch me out and to my punishment?* You extended past me and collected my used dishes, as if I could have bent the fork cleanly back enough to disguise its utility. In the dim light, even I could see the mangled angle of the bent prong.

Pathetic plans that never had a chance in this hell or any other. Yet I survived in the dark on these sad little fantasies. Breadcrumbs of hope. I enacted every detail in my mind until I felt that exhilarating wave of relief and freedom. Then I lived off that imagined reunion with my life.

After the fork disappointment, my mind turned to physically disabling You long enough to run. Yet You continued to only let me out for my bucket. Physical urgency captivated my attention when You released me, and shame left my resolve wilted when I was done. I just crawled back into my cage a little more broken each time.

I did not have the balls to face You, to challenge You in Your arena. I was only proved a failure, a victim of all my fantasies.

You knew. You knew all along. I was transparent to You. Apparent to You from the moment You pressed that cloth over my mouth. Maybe even before. I fooled myself, briefly, that I was being crafty and concealing my intentions. I told myself I was still my own person; I still had my secrets and privacy in my head. Gradually, even that illusion fell away. Then I knew that You knew.

After the fork, I told myself that maybe You did not notice. You had not reacted, aside from that sly smile of knowledge, and more importantly, You had not punished me. Yet on the one occasion I mustered the courage to feign a step at charging You, I caught a look in Your eye that dismissed the intention from my head.

Your eyes were not angry, and certainly not scared or surprised. Yet they were not lifeless and detached in purpose as they usually were. There was a depth and a connection in our brief eye contact that made me shutter. It was a semblance of an understanding I saw in Your expression.

You knew.

You would always know.

Somehow, You were deeper inside my head than I was even able to be now.

In that split second where our gazes mingled, my dream of escape wilted and died. You would always know; You would always be one step ahead of me. The hope that I had been sustaining shriveled up in my chest, leaving it feeling cavernous. My heart beat slow and hollow in the empty space.

A small part of my mind fell away, and I abandoned myself to mechanically following the routine.

Food and water.

The bucket.

Then again, You were gone. I was left alone, lying in a puddle of my ineptitude. Still trapped here. Still Yours.

9

I clung to my rage against my swelling and crushing despair. I felt the sorrow well up inside me, like a warm, thick, suffocating blanket, but I pushed back against it. I focused on the anger, became emotionally singular. I dug my nails in deep and clutched it close, along with the torturous visions of Lei, McAllister, even my office.

Julie's annoyingly warm smile and alarmingly chipper voice with my glorious morning coffee, steam curling out of the mug as the few drops of cream still twirled into the brown liquid.

McAllister tripping over his floppy puppy front paws while his back legs kept pumping, grinding his little nose into the grass before he realized to stop.

Lei singing softly to herself woefully out of tune while she kneaded elbow deep in a mound of dough.

Hold onto them. Hold onto that life. You're going back.

This was Your fault; You were doing this to me. You were keeping me from them, and I would get back to them. I would take my life back.

Fuck You.

Such silly fucking delusions. Rations I fed to myself to keep me from focusing on suicide instead. And Suicide was increasingly becoming a very tempting mistress. She lay down beside me in the dark, running her hand down my back like Lei used to do when I was exceptionally stressed. She whispered in my ear that she could make it end; she could make the hurting stop; she could free me from this place. More and more every dark day, she seemed the most compelling option to rescue me. Her embrace became heavier, more seductive.

If it wasn't for Lei's huge dark eyes that always appeared to dilate when she looked at me, even when she was pissed at me. Especially when she was pissed at me. If it wasn't for the thought of those stupid fucking bracelets on her soft wrist.

Between the sweet caress of the idea of flight through death and the haunting memories of my life stripped away, I felt insanity spreading through my cells, making a home in my chest cavity and skull. It felt almost comforting to exist with such abandon, to be at the mercy of my instincts and mental collapse. No worry of what a partner would think of me, no thought to what someone could use against me, no pretenses, no goals.

I simply was whatever the torrent in my mind fell upon at the moment. Waves of claustrophobia swelled in me and sent me crashing in a wild frenzy against the bars. Hopelessness dropped a black veil over my brain and reduced me to wasteful tears and sobs. Anger had me screaming until the sound of my own voice echoing back at me assaulted my ears.

My mind was a vengeful blur of images and emotions, a swirling tide growing stronger with each splat of those falling drops.

Drip, drip, fucking drip.

I shook the bars with all my might then softly cried myself to sleep. Day after day.

You were breaking me down. More brilliantly than I could realize, lost in my strife. You were leaving me alone to turn on myself, break myself down to something more pliable for You.

I wish I could have appreciated the beauty of it in my misery.

I couldn't take another day of it. I couldn't take another day of nothing but food dropped in front of me and being dragged to my bucket twice. I could not go on like this. Dogs had better lives.

The door moved; the light poured in. My body felt drained and redundant in this increasingly familiar and fluent dance of fear. Hours spent trembling against these bars quickly outweighed years lived on the outside; the resonation of distress through my cells was quickly becoming my baseline. I embraced it so easily; it infected my mind so effortlessly. For all I ever thought of my mind, it dissolved behind the beast at my core before I had the time to starve myself.

The room animated beyond my tomb. You hesitated in the wake of the door as usual, but You had a commanding presence that reminded me of my first night in Hell. You looked up, looked down at me again. I found excitement trimming the edges of my anxiety, and that, in itself, disgusted me.

Yet I could not help it. You broke the dark; You ended the isolation. With each passing second locked away, the fear and the pain You introduced me to seemed like the lesser of two evils.

I curled up over myself, folding my legs beneath me and wrapping my arms protectively around them. I put my back to the far bars of the small cage. I waited, almost rocking on my heels. You stood in the doorframe briefly, as before, then stepped forward.

You squatted beside my cage. I simultaneously wanted to press myself back through the bars to escape and to leap forward into Your lesson. The contradiction again surprised and disturbed me. I did neither. I waited silently on edge.

What the fuck does this mean?

As You reached in and dragged me out, I felt my fear rising. I would not feel this way; I would not be relieved to see You; I would not find comfort in Your presence.

I would hate You as I should.

As You yanked me to my feet and stood me in front of You, I felt my heartbeat quicken. Adrenaline was pouring through my veins; my muscles wanted to flinch. I stared down at the cement floor, noting the cracks I could see under the swinging light bulb and forced myself to breathe.

Hold on to the rage. Hold on to it. Fuck this motherfucker. Fuck him.

I steeled myself, forced her—that bitch hiding inside of me—to rise back up to meet my flesh.

Fuck this guy. Fuck this guy! I screamed to myself in my head until I could wrench my head up to meet Your eyes.

They were, in a word, terrifying. Your eyes were such a dark brown that they looked like two black holes in the middle of Your eyeballs. Holes that I could see taking me in and swallowing me whole. Holes that were empty and revealed nothing as to what You had tucked beneath all Your composure.

Now, my heart was literally pulsating against my ribs, sending vibrations through my skeleton. I was sure You could hear it. I had no doubt You could smell my fear, probably thrived on it.

"What the fuck do you want?" I spit the words in Your face, mustering all the ferocity and venom I could. "You going to fucking beat me again? Pussy."

The slap somehow surprised me. The blow was so clean and precise that my head snapped to the side. I felt my teeth sink into my cheek and tasted the iron flavor of my own blood on my tongue. My mouth hung open in shock.

"Like I said," I stuttered. "Beat me again, you pussy."

I was literally gagging on my fright, feeling my throat quiver and clench around every word. I didn't let it show; I forced it down away from my face and out of my voice. If I could hide being a lesbian for so many years, I could hide this. If I could be that office cunt every single day, I could fight You. I could give you the fight I should have had in me the first night I met You.

Your hand collided with my jaw again, exploding the same pain through my skull again. I felt it deeper; it throbbed harder. My nerves, my instincts were shrieking, *Retreat! Shut the fuck up!*

I did not speak again. I couldn't. My mouth was saturated with pain and the infectious taste of my blood. I could feel the ache radiating through my entire head, permeating my brain. I did not want the pain again; I could not ask for it again.

No. I could not just give up. I could not comply, could not submit. I could not let You win. How could I just let You after You took me out of my life, after You locked me in this awful fucking room, after You had me living like an animal, after You beat me senseless and left me to tumble into insanity? How could I accept that without a fight?

There had to be fight left in me. Somewhere.

I dug deeper, rooted around in my soul, if I still had one. I snapped my head up to face You and opened my mouth to assault You again. I even started to raise my hands. Fuck it, I would strike You, too.

You snatched my wrists hard, pinching until I felt my fingers tingle. You contorted my arms back until I felt the burning twist in my bones and muscles. I cried out and began to bend back to ease the pressure. You released one wrist and brought a fist smashing into my nose.

My sight exploded. I saw white then red then the swinging light again. My brain stuttered and flickered like movie off the reel before settling back on the sight of You standing over me. The anguish thumped across my face; each pulse of my heart raising the sensation. I could feel blood spilling into my mouth.

All thoughts of fight had been knocked out of my head.

I felt so weak. I felt so helpless. I felt claustrophobic again even outside of my small, metal box. The tears welled up over me as quickly as the pain had overtaken my body. I dissolved into blubbering. The convulsions shook my torso so hard I started to wilt before You. The anger and rage turned inward on me, burning hot down my cheeks. An avalanche of despair threatened to block out the small light above us. Thoughts were decomposing; coherency was abandoning me All that was left was the singularity of my depression, the weight of my hopelessness, the finality of my loss.

I didn't see the vicious punch to the stomach coming. I only felt the harsh impact and all the air forced out of my lungs. I tried to cough, but I was deflated. I no longer felt my face as the sensation detonated in my gut. My lungs burned as they groped to draw breath again. My abdominal muscles cramped tightly, forcing my body to wrap into itself. It was a heavy, sinking agony that drew me down into it. I simply relented and curled down around the pain until I felt the cold concrete on my skin.

You stood over me unmoving, but I knew it was ill-advised to remain puddled at Your feet. I heard my mother's voice in the distance. Dry it up before I bust your tail. I wanted to die right here. I didn't want to fight; I didn't want to snap to attention. I wanted my heart to stop beating and release me from this hell. I never wanted to see Your fucking face again.

The threat of more punishment menaced over me in Your eyes. I did not want more pain; I could not take more pain. I held my breath until the cries subsided; then, with my head buzzing, I dragged myself to my feet, stacked my feeble frame back up for You.

I stood silent before You with my obedient eyes cast down. I tried not to cradle my aching body. I tried to stand up straight as I stared at the floor. I was quivering on the inside, and my mind was consumed with the inventory of my injuries.

I just waited for Your next move.

A disgusting thought crept in and started to plague my mind: *Do what he says. Do what you need to do to live.*

10

In the darkness again, I cradled my pain. One hand rested on my cheek, where I could feel the stinging print of Yours on the curve of the flesh. The other hand wrapped around my tender and quivering stomach where Your fist had ignited my torso. I felt Your touches lingering on my nerves, as if You were still with me, on top of me in this tiny cage.

I didn't know if I was crying anymore. At this point, I don't know that I could tell. The messages from my neurons were crossed and convoluted.

Dry it up before I bust your tail.

Dry it up before I bust your tail.

It's okay to cry, Lei said softly into my hair. It's okay to have feelings, to let me see. I'm not going anywhere.

Their voices echoed off the concrete walls in my mind like so many phantoms and ghosts. The longer they raged, the less I could distinguish them from my own.

Do what he says. Do what you need to do to live.

That was me; that was my voice. And that silenced them all.

That fucking thought again. It felt dirty in my mind. It felt like a thorn in my brain tissue, like betrayal beneath my skin.

Just give up.

I dismissed it immediately of course. I physically bucked and pushed against that weak, pathetic idea. I didn't give up. I was a fucking tiger. I had just made my entire company my bitch. I was strong and capable. I took what I wanted. Even here penned up in a tiny cage, even stripped of all fight and reduced to blubbering in a couple of blows, I told myself these things. I slammed my hands into the bars.

"No!" I yelled to myself. "I won't!"

Desperation in my voice, trying to sell myself on my own bullshit, I thrashed against the bars again. I am stronger than this, I told myself. I can do this. But there it was, that tangible thought gently echoing in my skull, slowly infecting me. The crack that would eventually shatter me.

My body started screaming louder than me, louder than my mind. The beating was still painted on my nerves, reignited by my fit. I could feel the tears of defeat starting to well in me again as I wrapped my arms around my wounded torso and tried not to sniff through my damaged nose.

"No," I said to the bars.

"No no no no," I said against the drip. "NOOOOO!" I wailed at my cell.

You were going to hear me say no, even if I lacked the courage to scream it in Your face. I tried to bash and beat on and shake the cage, but my body didn't have the strength. My voice cracked as I screamed; it shriveled in my throat.

I was a shell of a human. There was a stranger seeping through my bones, infecting the marrow with doubt, with submission. I groped at my flesh, trying to claw it out, scratching to take handfuls of the disease, but it was too deep. Somewhere in my core, I knew the affliction was fatal. I could feel that former reflection of myself starting to rasp and rattle.

"Not yours!" I screamed. "Not yours! NOT YOURS!"

I fought it. I forced myself to shake the bars and tear the skin from my throat. You were going to hear me; You were going to hear me say no.

My entire body was pain now. My head throbbed from Your slaps mingled with my tears. My throat was raw from my fruitless and desperate shrieking. My ribcage captured the throbbing of my bruised abdomen and heaving lungs.

"No. No. Nononononono. No. No," I mumbled to myself incoherently.

No. I had to cling to no. No was the answer. No had to stay the answer.

I don't know why I believed I would be able to resist You. Yet I tried to claw my fingers down into the very idea.

I wanted You back in here. I didn't want to be alone. I wanted You to beat me so I could fight You, so I could prove to myself that I still was a fighter and didn't believe these nagging little thoughts. I wanted anything but to be by myself against the madness growing inside me.

That I could give up made me a stranger. That my mind had started to wobble made me a liability. That I could remotely want Your presence made me an enemy. Who the fuck was I anymore? Did I ever know myself at all if this was at my core?

Slowly, by degrees, I felt myself fearing myself more than I feared You.

Escape had ended in pathetic failure. Resistance seemed increasingly futile. Now what?

I breathed in deep, let the air stretch my wounded lungs; then a surprising sound tumbled out from my cracked lips.

"Ring around the rosies."

I heard my mother's voice. The way she would sing into my scalp and nuzzle her nose along the side of my face. It was smooth and warm, just like her breath teasing the hair by my ears. I closed my eyes, burrowed into her chest until I could hear her heartbeat keeping time with her lyrics, and felt safe.

"Pocket full of posies."

I wrapped my arms around myself, trying to simulate the feeling of her. My arms felt cold and foreign, lifeless like the steel and concrete enveloping me. I felt as dead as she was now. "Ashes, ashes, we all fall down."

The ragged lullaby and my own dead arms were oddly soothing. Or perhaps I was curled up in the comforting memory of her.

What would she think? What would she want me to do? Would she want me to fight until You beat the life out of me, or would she want me to bow, bend, play nice to make the pain stop?

Could she see me in this horrible fucking box?

The darkness stretched out in front of me the way I could not. I could feel the weight of the hours stacking up on top of me. Why had You left me so much longer? Why had You not come to let me to my bucket? Had You heard me screaming no to you? My body counted the drips. Then I felt the time accumulate in my bladder. It felt like every drop hitting the floor was gathering in a pressure on my pubic bone.

Damn that empty water bottle that left my mouth and throat parched. I could feel every drop in that bottle now pressing heavily on my urinary tract.

I squirmed at first, shaking my legs against each other, twitching my toes to distract my nerves. The cage was too damned confining. I started pattering the soles of my feet on the bars, tap dancing as hard as I could to think about anything else.

Hold it. Hold it. Hold it.

The tingling and the pressure mounted with each passing second, with each splash of that incessant drip. It was growing louder and faster; I was sure of it. I could feel the vibrations rippling through my engorged bladder.

Had You done this to me? Was this Your design? Another step in my humiliation. Another strip sheared off my humanity. Did You provide me the water then wait out the biological time?

My whole body was practically seizing. My inner thigh muscles were shaking, weak from holding so tightly, from fighting my own body. I screamed out without words and clenched my teeth, making fists until my nails dug into my palm.

As the hours ticked by with the count of the drips, I lost. I felt the warm failure flood my tiny prison.

11

When You opened the door, I was petrified. I didn't even look up to see You fill the doorframe. I simply shuttered in my own puddle, wept in my own shame.

I heard You inhale deeply through Your nose, hesitate, then sniff again.

You knew.

The sound of Your movements changed. I still refused to look. As if I could ever look up with pride again after wetting myself in a crate like a dog. Your shoes scraped the concrete rapidly; You tugged on the lock hastily. I hid my eyes with my hands like a scared child. I let my wet limbs stick to each other protectively. When Your hand wrapped around my ankle, anger was in the grip. Not the calm resolve and patience You had so consistently exuded.

I banged along the bars as You ripped me from the cage and chunked me aside on the floor, concrete slamming against my knees and elbows. I raised my arms around my head and curled into a wet ball, still whimpering, still sobbing.

I heard droplets fall from the blanket as You tore it out after me. It fell to the floor with a splat beside me. You reached down and took me by the neck. I felt Your fingertips sink in my flesh, constrict my arteries. My heartbeat throbbed in my temples. You heaved me to the blanket as I remained locked in a defensive fetal position, eyes squeezed shut.

I didn't want to know what was coming next.

You did not yell; You did not say a word. I could read the depths of Your rage and disappointment and contempt in the angry scrape of Your steps, in the force of Your grip, in the stiffness of Your breath. The sounds of Your body and composure spoke volumes to me and managed to unearth deeper fears when I thought I had been fully tapped already.

I didn't fight; I didn't move. I remained catatonic in my protective ball as You moved me. The smell choked me first. It was thick and pungent, acidic in my nostrils. My entire body shriveled in response as my throat tightened. I could feel my abdomen undulating in dry heaves. It was an unmistakable odor that I biologically rejected.

It was the smell of my own urine.

Then I felt the moisture on my face. My own piss spread over my skin as You cupped my skull and ground my nose into the soiled blanket, like disciplining a puppy that failed to be house broken. I coughed and sputtered against the fabric. My nose bent and contorted against the concrete beneath the blanket. I heard the cartilage crunch and grind through my sinuses.

My arms and legs shot out and flailed helplessly.

My hands slapped messily at the concrete. I tried desperately to stop breathing, to keep that scent and that taste out of my mouth. I didn't know humiliation could have such a distinct smell and sensation. This was humiliation; this was embarrassment.

This was me losing my humanity.

You pinned me down firmly for what seemed like an eternity, long enough for me to stop struggling, for me to fall limp and whimper in defeat. When I crumpled at Your feet, You finally released me. Your hand abandoned my scalp, and You yanked the blanket out from under me.

I gathered myself up, desperately scrubbing at my face with my hands, as You stormed out of my cell with my blanket and my shame. It took me a moment to notice You had left the door ajar behind You.

This was my chance.

Opportunity managed to infuse clarity into my muddled veins. I had to do this. This was my one chance to do this. It didn't matter what happened on the other side of that door; it only mattered that I *RUN*.

I scrambled sloppily to my feet, still in my soaked clothes, and lunged toward the light pouring in from the doorway. I could hear my bare feet slapping the floor. My hands were clawing out toward the freedom. My breath was panting through my lips. I could see my heartbeat in my peripherals.

I'm there. I'm almost there.

The four sprinting strides it took for the light to overtake my sight seemed to happen in slow motion. As my fingertips neared the doorframe, I heard a large thud on the other side of the door. The light collapsed on me; the door grew, and I felt the shattering impact on my forehead before the world went black.

I woke up in a pile against the closed door. My bruised nose butted up against the base, nearly tasting free air. I heard the knob turn above me and rolled out of the way before You opened the door again.

I was a failure at Your feet yet again. You were probably laughing to Yourself at how pathetic I was. Your demeanor had changed, reverted. Slow, methodic, calm, clear once again. I recoiled against my cage, huddling up against the outside of the bars, looping my fingers comfortingly through the thin metal.

You stepped forward until Your boots pointed at my bare toes. Fearfully, I looked up in Your direction but not at Your face. I couldn't bear to look You in the eyes. You set a stack of folded fabric on the top of my cage, took me by the shoulders, and stood me up in front of You. I came up to Your chest and stared blankly into the neat buttons trailing Your shirt. It was dark blue today. I don't think I had noticed a color besides black or gray since my first introduction to the dark.

You grabbed the sides of my pants and tugged them down around my ankles. Then You grasped the hem of my shirt and guided it over my head. I followed, like a toddler being undressed, yet it screamed in my head again.

RAPE! RAPE! RAPE!

I wrapped my arms around my bare body, felt my shrinking frame and loose skin in the air, and dropped my head. You didn't even look at my naked flesh. You reached down and unfolded a fresh pair of pants and held them out. I looked at them hesitantly, then sheepishly lifted my leg and stepped in, stabilizing myself on the cage. Then You pulled a loose and plain shirt over my head. My arms fumbled into the sleeves, then I cuddled into the feeling of clean clothes.

You unfolded the last piece of cloth and spread a new meager blanket into my cage. Then You stepped back and held the door open. I glanced at You then back to the floor before crouching down and crawling back in.

12

As I lay in the darkness, savoring the warm and dry sensation of fresh clothing and linens, I relived my punishment. I coughed at the memory of choking on my own urine. I shuttered in my arms at the anger I felt in Your touch. The pseudo-smothering changed my mind, slowed time itself. Everything became for vivid in those stuttering breaths. My body had been lost in the panic, but my consciousness had stepped apart, was able to watch You.

You had been so angry yet still so controlled. I could see it in every mannerism, in the way Your face contorted, in the way the tension quivered in Your flexed hands and arms. Your rage was palpable in the air so much that I nearly choked on it. Yet the punishment was less savage than even my introduction to this place. You hadn't beaten me senseless; You hadn't berated me mercilessly. There was a barrier, Your self-control between me and Your rage. You had tempered Yourself and disciplined me. You were teaching me. Your reaction had purpose.

It dawned on me that You were training me, like a dog.

The correlation of my cage to a crate, of my accident to housebreaking, of my imprisonment to ownership made me sick to my stomach. It brought a thin, acid taste into the back of my mouth. Yet it also made sense in a way that calmed something deep in my chest—just a little. I was figuring something out about You.

Perhaps, if I could discern what You wanted, I could make the pain stop; I could survive.

Did I even want to survive? Wasn't I just flirting shamelessly with Suicide in my cell? Couldn't I just defy You until You gave up and got rid of me? In my guts, I knew I did not have the courage for that surrender; I did not even have the courage to say no and face punishment, to stand up and be slapped down. I had no desire to find out how You would get rid of me, and I simply could not resign myself to dying here, in this cell. That foolish shred in me clung to the fantasy of seeing Lei again.

So if I wanted to live, I had to do what You wanted. But what did You want? I rolled the question around in my mind the way I twirled a pen through my fingers as I thought about what might hook a client's target audience.

He doesn't seem to have any interest in raping me, at least not yet. He doesn't want to kill me; he is investing far too much time in me. He does want to hurt me, but why? What does my pain get him? I didn't envision You shutting the door to my cell and jerking it on the other side. That seemed infinitely beneath You.

You wanted to train me; it was obvious You expected certain behavior out of me. It was also apparent that I had been nothing but a disappointment so far. Yet You still had not killed me. *He needs to keep me for something, but what? What is he training me for?*

What would my obedience give him? What need am I here to meet? What need will keep me necessary and alive long enough to get out?

Curling up in despair had left me the same in the dark. Escape plots were ambitious and unrealistic aspirations at failure. Maybe if I could just play along, I could make the pain stop. It tasted vile, like submission, in my mouth, but necessity often did. It felt disgusting to play straight and keep my private life tucked in the shadows to succeed at work, but I had done it to get what I wanted. Means to an end. And this was the greatest end. There was no carrot more seductive than the idea of freedom, than the simply base will to keep breathing.

I can do this; I can be what he wants. To stay alive. To lessen the pain.

Now I had to discern what Your cryptic nonverbal commands were demanding. I tried to dig through my dark and convoluted blur of memories from the past few days, or weeks, surely not yet months.

Most simply, You wanted me on a routine. Feedings and evacuations at the same interval every day. You wanted me on Your time; You wanted to control my world down to the basic, biological function. You also wanted to dehumanize me. Caging me like an animal, denying me light or speech, forcing me to piss and shit in front of You, disciplining me like a dog.

He wants to break me down, but why? To what purpose? If he doesn't sloppily get off on it, what is the point of owning another human?

I just could not stretch my mind around it. You remained largely a placid enigma to me. I told myself the deeper motivations were irrelevant. What mattered was the immediate, doing as I was "told," and making You happy enough to spare both the beatings and my life. If I played along, perhaps I could unearth Your more complex plans; perhaps I could progress into understanding.

I didn't have to understand to obey. All I had to do what read the commands and follow. Submit.

I tried to breathe the tension out of my muscles as

I pushed the resolve through my body. It felt foul permeating down from my mind and into my body. It felt foreign and unwelcome on my skin. My throat coiled into a ball, and sour saliva pooled in the back of my mouth. This was what I was doing, no matter how nauseated it made me. This was all I could do. At least I had a realistic plan now, not like my foolish musings at escape. This was the control I could have; this was the decision I could make.

Now I just had to wait for You and start behaving, start being whatever it was You wanted me to be. Yet You did not return at the normal interval, and the darkness grew around me. I lay alone with the dark with my dormant plan, with this idea unconsummated. It felt uncomfortable in my brain. I feared the longer I lay with it rolling around my skull, the more chance my body would reject it from its very core. I was forcing it down my own throat.

Means to an end. That is all it needed to be. My control. My choice.

My one chance.

I could do anything to get where I wanted; that was in my nature. That was how I needed to see it. *I am not forcing myself to be submissive; I am not relenting. I am just working another angle; I am exploiting another situation, giving the customer what he wants to get what I want from him. That is what I do.*

The idea calmed the sea writhing in my stomach. That manipulation on the truth settled my rampant brain. I took a deep breath to fill my aching sides and accepted it.

My mind relinquished the plan into the future, and as always, all mental roads led back to her. Lei walking in her bare feet on her toes through my thoughts, her flowing gypsy skirts trailing color behind her and teasing me with glimpses at her pale legs. I wanted to touch her skin. Even against those cold and lifeless bars, my fingertips still twitched in the memory at the way that smooth sensation would cause my eyes to flutter shut for just a second.

I just wanted to feel her arms encircle me. She would pull my head into her chest, even as I playfully resisted, until my ear was listening to heart gently rattle her ribcage. When she held me, she meant it. In every inch of her arms, in how her hips pushed forward against me, in the sound of her breathing me in. All I wanted, still alone in that cell, was that sensation. More than freedom, I just wanted her.

I would have given anything to not have felt so alone. To hear McAllister's panting in replacement of that vile dripping. To hear another human moving in normal patterns along the edge of my hearing peripheral. To feel anything soft. Lei was the epitome of all these things. Loud and bumbling through our rooms, unnaturally warm and supple, undeniably human and emotional.

Even if she had to fold into this cage with me.

I was a shitty partner. I loved her enough, but I never did anything with it. I let her die on the vine waiting for me while I chased a career that meant nothing in here. And here I was, wishing her into this hell with me, asking for her suffering to ease mine. She didn't deserve to be here like I did. Maybe she always deserved better than me.

She was everything You were not and, I would learn, would never be.

These thoughts of her were excruciating. They drew out such a deep longing from my very core that it felt like a knife gutting me deep and splitting me open. I felt my heart flayed wider each time I imagined her touch or hallucinated the sound of her jarring and endearing laugh. In this pain, I was amnesic to all her flaws. I would have bashed my head against the concrete walls encasing me just to hear her scream at me that she wasn't my priority again.

I would have that fight a million times to spare me a second in here.

Images and memories of her destroyed any calm or hope my resolve had kindled and plunged me back into those heavy hands of despair. Remembering her, what I did not have any more in here, made it all the worse. Her fucking warm skin, the fucking smell of the bakery on her, the fucking edge of her voice both annoying and charming, her big fucking eyes swallowing me up. That aching for her at my center dropped a weight on my chest, pulled me under the suffocating depression.

I thought I should push her from my mind. Again, to make the pain stop. I would take Your pain over the pain of missing her. I just could not let go of her. Yet.

13

The creak of the door and the invasion of the light at Your entrance was a welcomed break from the turmoil in my mind, the seething sea of memories and laments. I didn't want to be relieved to see You. I didn't want to feel anything but fear or disgust. Yet something else was growing up beneath those stock emotions, something deeper and more subversive.

I pulled myself up onto the balls of my feet, feeling the bars beneath the thin blanket. I poised my hands under me, squatting at the ready to crawl out to You. You knelt down beside my cage and took the lock in Your hand. You hesitated before releasing the latch, peered in through the bars at me. Your eyes were so piercing and unreadable. I felt them pierce through my own, burrowing into the back of my skull. Eye contact with you caused a physiological reaction in me; I felt my heart seize while my breathing fell quick and shallow. It felt like panic.

I don't know what I saw in Your eyes. I don't know what You were looking for in me. As usual, Your face was largely sedate and neutral, yet there was a flickering behind those eyes. We stared at each other for a breath, two; then the click of the lock roused us again.

You opened the cage door for me as You stood. I crawled out immediately, as I knew You wanted. I gathered my weak and unstable limbs underneath me before slowly ascending with my head low. It felt awkward to rise above the floor, to abandon the concrete I could feel radiating its cold into my cage at all times. I rose slowly, gradually, unsteady before standing and waiting, always looking down. I studied the gradient in the gray and the map of the cracks of the concrete floor and listened to Your breathing. Composed and controlled, gentle and natural.

This was not going to be a punishment like last time.

This was going to be something else. This was going to be my first true lesson.

Maybe it was excitement in Your eyes, something animating Your calm exterior. Your movements were deliberate but enlivened. I could barely hear Your footsteps drag along the floor as You picked them up lightly.

Your gloved hands gently took my wrists and guided me forward. I wanted to look up into Your face, explore it for more information, try to glean what it was You wanted from me. I was too scared, too intimidated. Every time my eyes threatened to venture up, the stinging sensation of having my face ground into that soiled blanket slapped through my nerves.

Like a dog flinching from the master who kicks him.

Another couple of steps forward across the small space, the concrete spreading beneath my bare feet. I pursed my lips and strove to keep my breathing level. I didn't want to reveal my pounding heart or my fluttering nerves.

Do what he wants. Just do what he wants.

I repeated it through my mind until it became my mantra. I thought the words until they began to lose meaning, until I could hear them in the sound of the drip. I just had to remain calm and figure out what You wanted to make it to the next day and the next day, in hopes that one of those days led me out of this cell.

At the lightest touch of direction, I lifted my arms to follow Your hands. The sterile, inhumane feeling of the gloves against my skin made me want to shrink back into my cage. Latex today. Everything was so cold and clinical in here, so detached.

You brought my hands together in front of You and began to bind my wrists. While Your eyes were down at Your task, I took the fleeting opportunity to look up and study You. I did so sheepishly, in punctuated glances, just in case You should catch me.

With Your head turned down toward my wrists, I saw the part in Your hair cut a crisp line down Your head, exposing Your pink scalp. Each hair was combed into place, beaten down by routine, not held down by product. The skin of Your neck and face had no blemishes, no scars, no dry patches, nothing. It stretched over Your bones tightly, even, and pale. Your skin looked like it would be soft, or maybe I just missed that sensation enough to start flirting with synesthesia.

With my wrists firmly hugged by their bindings, You let them fall against my body and stepped out of the cell. You knew I would not try to run again. The thought, of course, flitted up into my brain. Run. Just run. Yet I resisted it; I fought the urge rising in my cells and bubbling in my blood. A sprinting escape was a dead dream. I needed to keep to the plan.

You knew I would stand like a statue and wait for You. You returned with a plain metal stool, another dead piece at home in this box.

You withdrew the chain from its place on the wall. You slipped the hook on one end through my bindings then took a careful step onto the stool to loop the links through a ring dangling from the ceiling. A ring You no doubt mounted to this very purpose. Each connection in the chain bumbled and rang through the metal ring as You steadily pulled them toward You and hoisted my arms above my head.

With each clank and each inch, my limbs were heaved away from my torso. I felt further exposed the more I was extended, more vulnerable and laid out unprotected. My heart managed to twist and tense tighter still in this painfully slow dance, as You carefully posed me to Your liking.

Breathe. Breathe. Just do what he wants. Just get through it and do what he wants.

I knew You could hear the fear in my breathing now. I couldn't hide it or control it. My body was trembling from my fingertips teasing at the cold chain to my flinching toes pressing into the cold concrete floor. My muscles quivered below my skin; my organs shuttered inside my bones.

What was coming? I didn't know if I wanted to know.

Breathe. Breathe.

You stepped out once more, then returned with a small table and a tray of surgical instruments. Clearly, all of these items had been carefully staged just outside my cell in preparation.

Oh, fuck.

I began to shake so hard the links of the chain chimed against each other. My fear echoed in the small, bitter room. My mantra had lost all words and all meaning. Sense and planning dissipated in my mind, and only the base instincts surfaced out of the fog.

You were not affected by my deteriorating state. You did not acknowledge my emotions quivering on my skin. You simply kept to task, straightening the tools on the tray, pulling the table and the stool to the perfect angles.

I felt Your gloved fingertips lift my shirt to expose my midsection. My skin contracted from the caress of the air, from the exposure and vulnerability. Your hand then traced along the skin of my side. Not in a sensual or seductive way, more meticulous, more with purpose, searching for something. Your fingers slid along my rib, down around and over my hip, poking the skin, pulling it taunt. Then they settled, hovered over one section draping my hipbone. They swirled over and over in the same pattern, creating a light heat; then they retreated, and I heard You pull the instruments closer.

I didn't want to look. My eyes welled up with quivering tears out of sheer fear. They twisted and bent the light pouring down from above me; I wished they could twist and bend the stab of my terror. You wanted me to stand here and take it; You wanted something from that fleshy portion of my side. I had nothing to do with it; I was the stand to hold it up to Your purpose. I just had to make it through this. Then, perhaps, it would prove something to You, make me something worth keeping.

I felt the first cut split my world, sending pain ripping through my brain. Every muscle on my skeleton flinched, tensed, curled up around the anguish. I felt my opposite foot tapping at the floor, trying desperately to draw the attention of my consciousness away from the sensation. I could hear the bare skin slapping nervously against the concrete as I tried to concentrate on that cold sensation on the sole of my foot rather than the pain opening the side of my body.

The pain was so vivid crawling up my spine, as sharp as the scalpel parting my skin. I could feel the blood tracing the cut before spilling down the curve of my hip and soaking into the top of my pants. My body wanted to thrash and kick; a scream swelled my tongue. I felt my throat bulging with the sound as I nearly choked on it. I grasped at the shred of sanity being overwhelmed by the primal fight and flight, and I pushed. I shoved reason back down my throat, pounded my resolve through my veins.

Take it. Just take it.

My hands were clenching, trying physically to cling to the idea.

Take it. Just take it.

My fingernails dug into my palms until my fists quivered. I strained to focus my entire brain, to resurrect it out of the pain assaulting my nerves and bring it back to purpose. The flesh was so compelling though; its pleas infected my brain as organic as the thoughts I formed.

Why should I take it? How can I fucking take it? There is no way to please this motherfucker. It will never be enough. I will never be enough. He is taking my fucking skin. Taking it. Stealing it. Fuck this. I can't do this.

I had to pull my shit together. Collapsing on myself would not unbind my wrists or wrench the scalpel from Your hand. This was my only move; this was all I could do against You.

I choked in a breath through my own stifled cries and blinked hard until my eyes emptied down my cheeks. I needed to go somewhere else. Guided mediation and breathing worked for childbirth. Or so the straight women would tell me. If they could shove wriggling, splitting life through their vaginas, surely I could endure some unanaesthetized minor surgery.

I could do this.

The slice was migrating slowly around the curve of my side. My mind leapt to my mother. My eyes focused on the gravel covering the asphalt. *Sunlight blazed around me, and I looked down at my child knees to see the blood flooding to fill where the patches of skin had been scraped off. Grains of that gravel were imbedded in the wounds, and the burning sensation was starting to flare up and spread over my skin in goose bumps.*

I didn't move; I was paralyzed by the trauma. I felt only the panic and the pain, and I didn't know what to do with it. My ankle was still tangled in the frame of my fallen bike. I just curled my fingertips into my palm and wailed for her. I let the large tears plummet from my cheeks and the inarticulate sobs just pour from my tiny, quivering lips.

Nearly instantly, she was there, crouched down at my side. I didn't know how she could have gotten to me so fast, and I didn't care. She had cleared the house, front door, and yard after somehow picking up my cries over the radio she always had mumbling in the corner. I felt her hands fall onto my shoulders, and I felt safe again.

I continued to blubber though, too lost in the shock of the pain and the echo of the fall. She gathered me up into her arms, liberating my ankle, my blood streaking onto her hands and pants. She didn't notice or care. Her palm found my cheek as she hushed into my ear.

"Oh, baby girl, dry it up now. Your mommy's got you. No need for all those tears."

Her voice was always like a lullaby to me. Just the sound of it, the tone of it infected me with calm. I curled into her and smothered my cries until they faded. She absorbed them into her chest for me.

And we sat there in the gravel on the street, her rocking my pain away.

I held that warm and safe sensation in my chest as I resurfaced in Your prison. I fought to keep my mind on that street and away from what was being done to my side. I dug into that moment as buried as she was and clung hard to it.

Dry it up now. No need for all those tears.

I wanted my mother's arms around me now. I wanted to lose myself in the sound of her voice and the feeling of being burrowed into her chest. I wanted her to take me with her, even if it was into her cold grave.

Yet my mind could not ignore the relentless screams of my flesh. I could not keep myself clinging to that memory. My disobedient eyes wandered down. You were leaned in close to Your hand as it was administering the endless string of pain. Your other hand held my skin tight to be sliced open. You had drawn a diamond shape on my hip in my own blood, and it wept heavily.

You replaced the scalpel on the tray and leaned back to get perspective on Your work. You hinged back at Your waist and cocked Your head gently to the side, squinting before releasing Your eyelids again. Seeming pleased, You gathered up the forceps and scalpel.

You pinched the top corner of the designated shape between the forceps and began to tug it away from my body. Then, with the scalpel, You meticulously began to filet the skin from my hip.

My mouth dropped open in silent shock. You didn't even hesitate to observe my reaction. I did not matter here. My brain simply could not process what my eyes and my nerves were telling me.

The pain changed. The sharp carving spread, deepened, sunk in down to my bones and bloomed out across my stomach. My skin shrieked as You tore away its own part. I squeezed my eyes shut. I didn't know if it was worse to see what was happening or imagine it from the sensations screaming up from my nerves. My legs were weak and shaking below me, and my breathing was rattling desperate against my ribs.

My hip, where Lei rest her soft hand.

My hip, where McAllister pressed his slobbery snout.

My hip, where my mother tickled me relentlessly until I begged her to stop.

That was MY hip You were taking from me.

The blood flowed heavily as the wound widened. I could feel it stealing my heat and spilling it into the growing stain on my pants. I dared to look down. My head swooned at the sight; I had to keep looking away.

Anger flared beneath my scalp. I did not want to take it; I did not want to stick to my plan. Fuck You. You had snatched me off my stilettos and out of my life. You caged me, starved me, and beat me like an animal. You forced me to use that humiliating bucket and ground my face into my own piss. You kept me from her. Now, You were stealing my own flesh, the only thing I had at the bottom of that small cage.

FUCK YOU!

But I couldn't do it. I couldn't fight. If this was the pain when I complied, when I behaved, what would be the pain if I resisted? The fear of that was paralyzing. Would You skin my whole body with me chained here? I could sacrifice this small pound of flesh to not find out.

I could only curse You in my mind as I felt the meticulous slicing and tugging of You robbing me of my own body.

I do not know how long it took You to excise the little portion my skin. At some point, the endorphins swelled up in my veins and floated me off to incoherency. I slumped from my wrists and lay my head against my arm, whispering up to my elbow.

"I made it. We're finally here."

My eyes and my body grew heavier by the cut. I felt my body melting and my head falling back until I heard the instruments replaced on the tray.

You had finished. What was coming next?

I heard You stripping off Your gloves as You walked out the door. I was left trying to find myself again.

I could not bear to look down and see the piece absent from my side, the hole now in me. I fought the curiosity of my eyes, but I could not keep them from the instrument tray.

And the dripping strip of my flesh draped over it. It was thicker than I would have imagined, marbled with the fresh blood. There were no words for what it looked like separated from my body. Something about the very sight brought my stomach into my throat. I choked back a heave and forced my eyes away.

I began wailing from my core, the sound shaking my entire ribcage and the teeth in my gums. I could not contain it. I wanted my skin back. I wanted out this place. I wanted You dead. Hopelessness swallowed me like the sea, my inarticulate laments raged like the crashing tide.

How could I live through this?

You returned, calmly unaffected by my cries. You removed the instrument tray, and the piece of me, from the room. With fresh gloves, You brought in a new tray of gauze, alcohol, medical tape. Then You unrolled a thick mat onto the floor and unfolded surgical pads over it.

You were infuriatingly placid, maddeningly scrupulous. I wanted to know what the fuck You were going to do with MY skin. I wanted to kick You in Your smug, stoic face and carve out one of Your eyeballs for You to see. Yet I only hung there, depleted and whimpering, watching You prepare my recovery suite on the floor.

I half expected You to chuck me bleeding back into my cage. I half wanted You to, if I could bleed out from sectional skin removal.

Instead, carefully stepping around the edge of Your perfect padding, You gently released the chain and lowered it, clinking link by link, until my arms draped heavily back along my torso. You abandoned the chain still dangling through the loop on the ceiling and slowly unbound my wrists, cradling my knotted hands in one gloved palm as the other hand skillfully liberated the cord.

My hands had given up and gone numb long before, when my legs, and my resolve, began to fail me. As I concentrated and turned them over each other, needles assaulted my skin in rising waves. Even with the gaping hole in my side still bleeding, I grimaced at this discomfort.

You took my hand in Your glove. I was so startled by the mild gesture that I nearly recoiled. You placed Your other hand on my back and guided me toward the mat. I simply followed, complacent and bewildered, internally flinching.

I felt my shoulders slump and my body subtly coil protectively inward. I felt my eyes shifting nervously from side to side. I felt myself cringing away from Your soothing touch. You ignored my foolish twitching and led me onto the center of the pads.

My mind was seized with confusion. I was questioning all of this, but I was not forming thoughts. It was just a fog of blurred emotions shifting across my consciousness. I felt my primal fear and let that speak to me. I let my resolve to just do as I was told guide me.

You tapped the top of my shoulders to instruct me; I collapsed at Your feet. You squatted in front of me and softly pushed me; I tumbled onto my unwounded side, still softly sobbing, still with wide, untrusting eyes.

Surely, You weren't kind enough to just kill me now. Suddenly, surviving long enough to escape didn't seem so necessary.

After several seconds ticked by void of violence, I released my clenched muscles. I wrapped my arms around my chest. I tucked my legs in closer. I closed my eyes and cried silently. If I could have curled into a shell, I would have happily lost myself there. I only felt the throbbing chasm of agony vibrating on my side, the nerves pulsating all the way up into my brain.

The pain was fluid, flowing and pouring between my skin and my brain, captivating my entire biological attention. Physical injury infected my emotions, and I felt the bottom drop out of my chest. I felt that hopelessness rise out of the darkness below. I let the flame of my light flicker low.

I heard the cap of a bottle unscrew, the swirl of swishing liquid. Then the stinging on my side ignited. The world went red behind my eyelids. My limbs shot out, and I howled wildly. You placed a hand on my shoulder to hold me, to calm me.

Your hand was soft and heavy on my nerves. It stirred a strange and now foreign emotion below all the turmoil. It was comforting; it did calm me. It felt familiar, forgotten, missed. Then You made a sound.

You hushed me.

Like a parent to a frantic child. Like my mother into my hair on that street.

I breathed, breathed, strove to rein myself in. I breathed the tension out of my muscles slowly, by degrees. I brought my limbs cautiously back into my body. I relaxed my face and rested my head on my folded arm. The sting of the cleaning cloth shook the bones in my pelvis, bled across my skin through to the other side. The air licked fire onto my open wound.

You did not stop. Your glove remained on my shoulder until the tension in my limbs faded. You dabbed and swiped the cloth slowly, methodically, softly until the hemorrhaging slowed and the surrounding skin was clean. The concentration of the hurt dissipated slightly with each swipe as my nerves became accustomed to it, as the alarm faded from my system. I had to strain less and less to fight off the tension. You tilted Your head to observe Your work again, gauging the speed at which the blood droplets welled. Then You took gauze and tape and carefully dressed my wound.

With Your hand under my shoulder, You sat me up on the mat. Your arm reached around me with Your palm turned upward. Several pills were cradled in the center. I did not hesitate. I gathered them in my fingertips and tossed them into my mouth. You handed me another plastic water bottle to chug them down. The large pills clung to my throat, but I pushed them down hard.

I didn't even stop to question what they were.

You stood me, properly bandaged, back up on wobbly legs. Concealed from the air, the injury's shrieking had been muffled to a steady, heavy ache. I was feeling unsteady and lightheaded. Utterly drained. The way I felt after torturing myself at the gym until I saw spots or after crying myself into dehydration. Maybe this was a bit of both.

My head was starting to swim. Somewhere between the adrenaline hangover and whatever was gradually seeping into my bloodstream. I was falling back away from my nerves, away from my body, retreating exhausted. I barely felt You exchange my bloody clothes for fresh ones. I scarcely noticed being tucked back into my cage. I only found myself curled up in the dark with my own hand resting protectively on my bandage.

I did not accept it then, but that night, I became Yours.

"Not yours," I still whispered to myself as a heavy sleep crept in through the bars.

14

The only thing that existed when I peeled open my puffed eyelids was the pain in a diamond shape on my hip. There were no walls, no bars, no drip. Nothing but that missing patch of skin, nothing but the nerves and capillaries calling out from the flesh carved away. My hand was still on top of the bandage, wet now with the warm blood seeping through.

My head felt empty, and my tongue cleaved to the roof of my mouth. My nerves were unmedicated again; I felt again.

I didn't want to.

I told myself it was morning because I had just woken up, but it was only dark. I told myself it was morning because it would feel normal to wake up into a morning. Who knew how long or short or skewed my "days" had become in this box? At some point, it became the least of my worries.

So I just told myself it was morning as I cradled my wound.

This morning, You appeared at the regular interval. Under the swinging bulb, You again assembled my recovery suite. You unrolled the mat onto the floor again, then unfolded surgical pads over it. You placed a tray of gauze, alcohol, medical tape beside it. It was identical to the night before. Every time would be identical.

Instead of the plate and the bucket, we began this day with wound care. You took the edge of my bandage between Your gloved fingers and slowly peeled it back, exposing my injury, taking the top layer with it. The air bit hard at the tender flesh, if it could even be called flesh in this state. I managed to keep my limbs clenched in at that first bite of the alcohol. I could hear my strained breaths fighting to exert control over my body.

Your untasked hand again found my shoulder; You again hushed me softly. And I again found some measure of comfort in it, something to get me through the sensations pulsating through me.

I was not bleeding this time, so I required less cleaning. You tilted Your head and squinted Your eyes as You swiped that alcohol repeatedly over the budding scab. We would begin a long string of days with wound care, until my body began to patch and stitch itself back together with sloppy, shiny new skin.

I was relieved to stretch out from the cage and spread myself onto the padded mat. I could appreciate laying out, truly laying out. The blood throbbed down into my limbs, pumping freely and expanding seemingly collapsed pathways. My muscles uncoiled stiff and depleted, inflating with the free- flowing blood and awash with endorphins. After however long of being folded up against those bars, my bones almost forgot the bliss of being extended.

Maybe this is worth a little flap of flesh. I caught the thought as it levitated up from my happily humming limbs. Could I actually consider selling a piece of my own skin for these oases on the mat? Is that what I had been reduced to? And did I care with how wonderful it felt at this moment? I had not had one ounce of joy since my last footfall in that parking lot. Any measure of it was vastly becoming worth my soul.

Then the antiseptic bit again.

You nursed Your work with such care. I could tell You were proud of what You had done to me, how it reflected back in Your eyes even with Your calm and slack features. It was something glimmering in Your eyes that I caught only when I snuck quick glances while You were distracted by the task. An animation, a light around those dark irises.

I shoved the burning sensation aside and focused on the calm rapture of being out of the cage and being cared for. My body felt whatever measure of free I could conjure in this place, but more Your gentle care bordered on nurturing. A sensation my soul itself was starving for. I didn't want to like it, but I found that I loved it. It was a vacation from my life in this cell. It was a fucking pleasure cruise from the dehumanization and the beatings. I could almost see You as a human in this light, even though I was sure You were investing in Your creation more than my survival or well-being.

Details.

As You took Your sweet time, I closed my eyes and did likewise. Basking in the light of the weak bulb, I imagined I could feel the warmth of the sun. I had almost forgotten what the sun looked or felt like at this point. I doubt my pupils could have taken its intensity, but I could ignite it above me safely in my mind.

I conjured up the memory of Lei walking down the topless beach in Sint Maarten, hips swaying, breasts bobbing, stomach enticingly flat and tanned. My mouth salivated for her as much as it did for the coladas she held sweating in each hand. The trip we took when I made senior associate, the trip I planned to calm her incessant nagging about when we could buy a house. She had abandoned all her resentment and all her disappointment and looked at me with only love in her eyes for that long weekend.

Her hair was kinked in dried salt water. Her skin was colored by the long affection of the sun. Her eyes were as bright and her face was as free as when I first met her in the coffee shop in the lobby of my marketing internship. She was perfect in those days, and wallowing in that memory made my heart ache more than my gaping wound.

I missed her in my soul, which suffered so much more exquisitely than this withering body.

Maybe my nerves would eventually die out. A girl could dream, spread out on this mat covered in surgical pads like a beach towel.

You sat me up again. You spared me Your soiled gloves and brought Your naked palm around me, cradling my next dose of medication. I felt myself wanting to lay back into You, wanting that arm to wrap around me comfortingly. You did not permit me to touch You though. Instead of holding Your hand out for me to gather, You waited until I offered mine and dumped the pills into my palm. After You handed me the water bottle, You signaled for me to stand. I followed direction. My heart sank when You next gestured at the bucket.

That fucking bucket.

However, You made the command then left the room. Left me alone out of my cage. Left me alone in the light. Left me alone with a shred of privacy and decency.

Somehow, it almost felt human to evacuate into a bucket when I was alone.

You returned with the plate and bottle of water, and I climbed back into my cage without a gesture, cautiously feeling more like a possession than an animal. I could endure this other side of You. I could be the pet You cared for; I just didn't know if I could also be the pet You kicked to earn it.

"Thank you," I whispered quietly.

The words escaped my lips before I could stop them. My voice did not even sound like my own as it escaped my dry mouth. What the fuck was I thanking You for?

You froze as You shut my cage door. Just for an instant. You looked down, and I saw a smile tug Your limp cheeks. You seemed to drink in the sound of my words for just that second; then, stifling Your reaction, You latched my lock and shut the door behind You.

I was still stunned at myself. My mind was dangling agape in the dark, hung on the last vile syllable. *Thank you? Fucking thank you? To the animal who just sheered a tender and cherished section of my own flesh. What in the sweet fuck?*

Yet I had felt it when I said it. I was thankful for the clean bandages, for the time alone and out of my cage, for the meager meal. I did not know how I could be thankful for such shit, yet the sensation poisoned my chest just the same. It felt uncomfortable and foreign, like a blade.

I wriggled against the feeling, disgusted by it. Yet there it sat, sunken into my center like a cancer.

The crisp bandage almost felt like a new life. The simplest of changes to my circumstances were earth-shattering now. I never knew I could savor clean clothes or dressing so much. I had to find anything that was less than misery where I could, and today, I found it in a kind touch and a clean swatch of gauze.

I curled up on my side, again placing my hand gently on top of my wound. It felt safer to cradle it, though the pressure on the sensitive and raw nerves encouraged the constant ache. I let the pain spread over me like a sheet on top of my inappropriate comfort, and I let it lull me to awkward sleep.

How could I sleep at a time like this? How could I ever sleep in a place like this?

Yet I tumbled out from the bottom of my cage and back onto the warm sand of that beach, back to being transfixed by the way her body moved in the sunlight bouncing off the waves. I felt my own body peak just looking at her, the way she was smiling at me behind her ridiculously large sunglasses.

"Isn't it nice to actually be on an island this time?" *she laughed as she flopped herself down on the chair beside me. I shamelessly watched her breasts bounce as she landed.*

"Well, naturally, this is better than being in the hospital," I replied.

"You should have just told them what was happening."

"I didn't need them knowing, didn't need those other vultures using it against me."

"Just like you don't need them knowing you have a girlfriend at home. It was just a hysterectomy. How could they hold that against you?"

"You'd be surprised. No one asks questions about a vacation to the Caribbean," I said, taking her hand. "Let's not talk about that now. We're here now. For real. Me and my girlfriend at home."

She slipped the slick glass into my free hand as she leaned in and pressed her lips to mine. She opened her mouth, and I would have taken a handful of her skin right there on that beach if I had a free hand.

My unexpected youthful hysterectomy. Another offensive thing for which to be thankful. After the urine incident, I could not imagine how a monthly pool of blood would have been met.

As consciousness licked at the edge of my dream, I tried to push it back, attempted to reject it. I could live forever in the memory of that beach. I wanted to taste the dried salt on her lips. I wanted to smell the sweet Guava berry colada on her breath. I wanted to search for her eyes behind my reflection in her sunglasses.

But she faded from me. The sunlight died in my mind as the claustrophobic darkness poured back over me. I opened my eyes into black. Once reality rose to the surface, the dream dissipated as if it had never graced me at all. I could only escape in sleep or in Your gentle aftercare.

Again, it was the dark and the drip and the solitude.

My heart felt like an aching hole again in the wake of thoughts of her. She filled my chest then left it horribly deflated, throbbing, and empty. The more I wanted her in every fiber of my body, the more I gradually started wanting to forget her. I couldn't have her, and by the dark minutes ticking by, it felt more like I would never have her again.

That realization, and the more true it felt as I rolled it around in my brain, tore me down my center, ripped me apart from the inside. I would have taken another flaying over feeling void of her.

I had taken her for granted. The realization cut even deeper. Why had she stayed through so many broken promises? Why had she waited and waited for me to make it? Why had she hitched to my career wagon and just followed where and when I chose to lead? She had to want more than just a life settled down with me and McAllister. Where was her drive? Where were her dreams?

Did I really know her at all?

I didn't want to think about it. I wanted to preserve her as perfect in my mind—untouched and untainted by being with me. I didn't want to think about all those nights she waited on the couch for me, McAllister laying against her legs with his head nuzzled on her hip, and all those nights she would be there now.

I was relatively sure I was never coming back. They certainly had stopped looking for me. My hair was brushing against my neck now; it had been too long. Maybe she had given up on me, too. Maybe it was like I never existed at all.

Was someone new sleeping on my side of the bed? Someone who came home promptly every night and gave her all the attention she deserved.

I wondered when they noticed I was missing at the office. Lei would have noticed the next morning. No matter how late I worked, I was always in bed with her by the time she woke up. An unexplained absence from me was unheard of and unprecedented. Julie would have noticed by 8:15, been worried by 8:30. I imagine, at first, she would have been relieved to not be chasing down my coffee and heading my direction. Then perhaps sometime before lunch, she might have become legitimately concerned. Maybe I had gotten into a car accident. I was never too sick to work from my bed.

After a few days, despite all the concern they faked, the office would begin to doubt me. Rebecca, the other partners. People like Denise and Andrew would be secretly celebrating, plotting how to consume my clients and cannibalize my success. Greedy bastards. Denise would show up in Rebecca's office, hand on her heart when she talked about how tragic it all was, offering to help out with my accounts in any way she could. Andrew would swirl a straw in his coffee cup in the break room, saying how he thought I just ran off; I couldn't handle the pressure.

But I had cut their metaphorical throats, hadn't I? Did they deserve it? Yes. Would they have done it to me? Without hesitation. Yet here I was in this box. Here I was being tormented, punished while they continued on their ruthless little lives. Why did they get to continue on free?

Did I deserve this?

Was this the price of my success? What success was ever achieved if it wasn't ripped from someone else? You couldn't win without competition, without crushing your competition.

Somehow, randomly, my mind surfaced on my first. The first time I crossed that line, the first small infraction where I chose myself at the price of another. It was small, of course, but it was the start. Maybe the first step on the path that led me here.

"Beatrix, can you step into my office, please?" Mr. Anders said from the other side of my cube wall.

I felt my nerves ball up into my chest. I knew why he wanted to talk to me. The proof to BareEssentials was incorrect, a typo glaring in the slogan. Your only as beautiful as your makeup. I hadn't noticed it until the delivery confirmation had arrived. My heart had plummeted into the pit of my stomach with the paper in my hand.

I knew I was fucked. I knew I had destroyed my chances at this internship. This was my toehold, my foot in the door into marketing, and I had wasted it on bad copyediting.

My hands were trembling. I clenched them in and out of shaky fists as I forced myself to take a deep breath. It was time to face the music and bid my career aspirations good-bye.

"Yes, Mr. Anders," I said as I emerged from my cube and followed him into his office.

He gestured to the chair and shut the door behind us as I gingerly sat down. I couldn't even fake confidence at this point; I was so crushed by my own stupid failure. I was already planning my pity party—liquor store and pizza on the way home to cry myself to sleep.

"Beatrix, have you seen the BareEssentials proof?" he said as he sat behind his desk. His brow was folded thickly, wrinkles deepening. He coiled his hands in front of him, and I saw his skin whiten at the pressure.

What to say? What to say? Should I just confess now? "I worked on it, yes," I replied ambiguously.

"The goddamn slogan is wrong!" he yelled, then composed himself. "Your only as beautiful as your makeup? Your! Like we don't know fucking grammar! BareEssentials is livid. They're dropping the contract. This is a huge loss for us. A huge loss."

He stopped for a moment. I could feel that my eyes were wide. I could feel my hands clutching the armrests of the chair. I was waiting for the axe to fall. He lifted his hands to his brow and massaged the deep wrinkles, swirling the skin around his forehead.

"What I need to know from you is, did Nancy sign off on this before you sent it?"

Nancy was the gatekeeper, the last link in the chain before something was released to a client. She reminded me of my mother, the way she could seem nurturing and ruthlessly sassy at the same time. She brought donuts to put in the kitchen one Monday a month.

When I had brought the proof to her, she was drowning in work. Stray hairs had wriggled loose from the bun tied on the back of her head. She leaned on her hand with her wide eyes frantically scanning the stack of papers fanned out in front of her.

"Sorry, dear," she said when I approached her. "Grocery- Mart wants to review contracts from two

years ago. It's just a mess in this file. You need a signature? Here, hand me the sheet. I trust you."

She scribbled her name on the sheet; I thanked her and sent the proof.

"Yes," I told Mr. Anders quietly, looking at his hands folded again in front of him instead of into his eyes.

"Thank you, Beatrix. That's all I needed to know. Get back to your desk and just make sure you, and everyone else here, double and triple checks every proof from now on."

Nancy had been fired that night. Taking her family photos and the pictures her grandkids had drawn home in a sad, plain box they provided her.

I hadn't thought about Nancy in years. I had not wanted to relive it. I didn't throw her under the bus or slit her throat. She had made the mistake—of signing a proof without reviewing it, of trusting me. Yet I hadn't confessed either. I had let her go down so that my career could continue.

My first trespass. The beginning of my self-serving aspirations.

Maybe I did deserve to be here.

But how would You have known all this? How would You have chosen me to punish me for all these sins?

You clearly had chosen me. You obviously had a purpose for me. But what? If You didn't know my less than innocent past or career path, if You weren't privy to the way I wasted Lei, why me? What were You punishing me for if You didn't know my crimes?

How did You choose me? The question was like a thorn nestled in the rear of my brain, constant and ruthlessly annoying. Was that You side-eyeing me over a coffee cup as I screamed oblivious into my dear cell phone and pounded the pavement with the spike of my heels? Was that You smiling as You handed me a receipt for my secret cigarettes? Was that You offering to buy me a drink in a shifty tavern before I snarled rejection at You? Did You see me with her? Did You know my life as intimately as You controlled it now? Was I just some random acquisition, or did You meticulously select me? I could not place You in my former life. I could not see You stalking that alternate reality, but I could not see You making any rash or impulsive grab at Your desire either.

How many nights did You wait for me in that parking lot? Why that night? Why me at all?

More questions to which You owned all the answers. I told myself that You studied me, that You closely evaluated me and compared me to others, that You saw something special in me. It was the only thing that could make sense, with the way You conducted Yourself, with the work You were investing into me. In my mind, You constructed this world just for me. You fantasized about bringing me here until that fateful night.

Every person had a motive or an angle. Every client wanted to sell something. What did You want?

You did not want my fight. You wanted to break me of that and force me into compliance. You did not want my pain. That seemed collateral to Your underlying motives.

You wanted my submission.

There was only one thing left for me to try.

15

It was my shame. My disgusting, pathetic last resort. My misguided understanding of submission.

As I heard You enter the room, I took a deep breath all the way in the bottom of my lungs. I let it stretch out my chest until it felt like it might burst. I poured myself into that one breath, attempting to calm my nerves and focus my purpose.

I could do this. If it would work.

You opened the cage door to lead me to my bucket. I crawled out cautiously, ever minding my still tender wound. I did not shuffle across to the bucket though. I took another breath and, instead, I stood before You. I could not look up into Your eyes. I stared as boldly as I could at Your scuffless, perfectly laced shoes.

I could do this.

You nudged me toward the bucket, but I resisted, tensed my body to hold myself still. I could feel myself starting to tremble from the muscles against my bones radiating out to my skin.

It had to be done. It had to be at least tried.

I turned to face You. The contact of Your dark eyes was petrifying. My irises fought against me to dive back to the safety of the concrete. Another deep breath. I forced myself to keep looking at You, to find some sort of terrifying connection with You, to try to make You see me. Then I dropped my eyes and lost myself in my respiration again.

Deep breath.

I lifted my hands with fingers quivering like leaves. I focused hard to steel the digits and keep them under my command.

Deep breath.

I began awkwardly tugging at my clothes, my shaking fingers sending ripples through the cloth. I could feel my whole body tremor outward then down into my core.

Deep breath.

All the breathing was doing nothing to calm or progress my efforts. I couldn't look back up at You now, not while I was doing this; I couldn't convincingly sell my seduction, but I had to try.

Sex had to be the answer, had to be what I could sell for the key. Sex would be the ultimate submission, me giving You the only part of me I seemed to still control, the only part You were not going to take. So I offered it to You.

I thought I heard a laugh swirl into Your breath. I thought I heard a small smile stretch Your thin lips. You simply reached down and grasped my hands. Your gloves were already on, and I felt the inhuman material cradling my quivering hands. You held them in Yours for what seemed like a long moment as You pulled them from my clothes. You turned me and guided me to the bucket, then returned me to my cage and my solitude.

As I heard the lock click and watched the light dissipate, I realized that I did not understand You at all. I had no idea what You wanted, and even if I was right about the submission, I clearly did not know what it meant.

You never touched me that way, despite all my fear. You never cared that I was a lesbian, or a woman for that matter. I don't think the thought even crossed Your mind the many times You peeled the sweaty, bloodstained clothes from my body. That sort of depravity was beneath You. You were creating a new life, not stealing sex. You didn't need that sort of pathetic display to establish Your power and control. Any violence You showed me was a lesson; it was merely a tool wielded to contour and break me into Your quivering masterpiece. I was simply and purely a human possession.

I think then You knew I was broken. When I offered You the last thing I had, You knew I was Yours.

When You returned for my feeding, it was like my sloppy and sad offering had never happened. Your face was as neutral and unreadable as ever; Your mannerisms and movements were as mechanical and purposeful. You let my embarrassment and rejection just drift out of the cell and memory.

I could almost consider that a kindness, and I could almost be thankful to You for it.

Your rejection tilted my perceptions of You. Something about You not being willing to ravage me, consensual or not, made me feel safer, made You feel more human. Even remembering the strap, the piss-soaked blanket, the scalpel. Even with all these torments and offenses, this one sanctuary revealed You had standards. There was pain and suffering You were not pursuing; there were things You did not want. This proved You had a purpose and were not acting on savage impulse.

Somehow, that was more comforting than it should have been.

As I ate slowly in the dark, my mind wrestled over itself. My thoughts were chaotically conflicted as my emotions surged lost through my veins.

He didn't take me. Why didn't he take me? Isn't this what this is about? Why else would you lock a woman in a cage? What more submission can I give him?

Rape is not what this is about. He spared me that. This is about something more. He has some kind of plan, some kind of purpose for me. *He wants something more from me, more than my body. He sees me as something more.*

Feeling gratitude toward You, appreciating anything about You, greatly assaulted the deep, writhing hatred I harbored toward my captor and torturer. I felt myself turning on myself and aligning with You as the thoughts infected my own brain.

As the hours passed in this small box, as the days washed over me in the dark, I was seeing the worst of myself, the more I deserved this fate, and the better of You, the way all of Your torment had an intelligent design.

The ideas were foreign and still disgusting to the small shred of self I had cradled deep below my heart. Yet they were mounting, growing, and spreading, being reinforced by the silence. *He sees me as something more. He has some kind of plan, some kind of purpose for me. I mean something to him.* They kept repeating and building. No one was here to contradict or correct me. No one was here to save me. It was me alone against Your eloquent conditioning.

Maybe You didn't fuck me just to elicit this turn in me. Maybe it was all part of Your plan. Even with that realization in my mind, it was still working.

A long string of days snaked through my cell quiet and uneventful. It took me several rotations through the bucket and plate routine to realize You were permitting my gaping wound time to heal. You weren't trying to destroy me; You were ensuring I recovered properly before enduring more. From the way the red retreated back into my wound rather than advancing across my skin, You were clearly feeding me antibiotics. And some glorious variety of painkiller. More planning, more consideration.

Each day, the light cracked my world open and announced You. Without a word, You knelt beside my cage. I felt the exhilaration of You being in the room, my heart pounding as You were so close to my space, as if the bars under Your fingertips were my own skin. You turned the lock, and the quiet release echoed through the room.

You placed the plain, metal plate at my feet and watched as I clumsily turned to face it. I looked up at You cautiously then waited for You to shut me back into the silent darkness before I gingerly nibbled at the plain chunk of bread or piece of undetermined meat. I tried not to attack it ravenously, attempted to temper my hunger and behave and ration.

The routine repeated for my second meal. You permitted me my two visits to my bucket, thankfully across the room, in the dark corner out of mind. With so little intake, I barely filled the bucket anymore. However, I waited for my designated time, like a dog crated all day while his owner is at work. Months of conditioning and that one harsh lesson taught me to not dare to soil my space, to train my bladder and bowels. Like a dog crated all day. My body learned to dance to Your rhythm long before my mind relinquished and fell in step.

And in this isolation, I started to want You. I didn't notice it at first. It was something new welling in my chest, something I did not recognize. You came into my cell, as the normal routine, yet as You reached in to deposit my feeding or to escort me to the bucket, I found my muscles were no longer flinching. I no longer curled away from You in anticipation of pain.

With no fresh lessons, the fear started to fall dormant inside me.

The next time I lay alone in the dark, I felt the need rising in me, swelling up in the vacant space in my chest. I wanted You there; I wanted Your care. When You came in to unlock my cage, my heart quickened. It was excitement maybe, not fright. I sat up, coiled my limbs beneath me. I moved my head, tried to entice Your gaze, tried to engage Your eyes.

You denied me. You left me wanting.

I breathed into my loneliness, even in Your presence.

The silence continued and felt heavier on me than it usually did, more empty. I wanted the soft edge in You when You were treating my wound. I wanted that concentrated attention. The squeak of my cage door whined through the quiet, drowned out my own sad breathing for just an instant. Your arm broke into my plane to deliver my meal.

"Thank you," I said quietly.

Again, the words escaped my lips before I could purse them down. Why was I saying it again? Did I mean that? Was I thankful? Or did I just want some kind of reaction, any kind of interaction with You? My voice was hoarse, unpracticed, and unrecognizable. As haggard as my physical body and as tragic.

You did not respond this time. No hesitation or even a hint of a smile. It was like being cared for by a robot.

My heart sank into the black in my chest as the darkness consumed the room behind You. I didn't bother to eat or reach for the water. I did not care. Again, I managed to feel heavy and more alone, neglected, and forgotten.

The fact that I had been reduced to wanting You disgusted me to my very core, yet it persisted below my skin just the same. I curled up with it as I forced myself to sleep.

In my feverish dreams, it was not Lei who greeted me. It was You. You were infiltrating and polluting my subconscious; You were staking Your territory into the deepest recesses of my mind. I had nothing of my own anymore.

You walked into my cell without hesitating. You did not stand in the doorway; You did not look down at me from the sides of Your dark eyes. You moved to my cage with purpose and loosed the lock quickly. You did not make me wait for You. Both of Your hands broke through the door. You did not guide me; You reached for me, taking my hands in Yours, no gloves between us. The heat of Your fingers tangled in mine raced through my body. You led me out of my cage, unfolded me, and pulled me to You. You held me to Your firm chest as You hushed into my hair.

I woke up heaving, cold, alone, and crammed between the bars of my box. Had I eaten the last meal You laid at my feet, I would have vomited in my cage. Instead, the acidic wretches just shook my empty frame.

Then I heard the door. I caught the gag in my throat and swallowed it back down, air contorting in my stomach. I wiped at my mouth with the back of my hand, somehow scared that You would be able to read the vile dream on me.

You entered my cell differently, more familiar. You were engaged once more. Your posture had purpose.

Your eyes finally fell on me again, examined me, and I recoiled from their intimidating contact once again.

I felt myself basking in Your attention, in You actually looking at me. I was happy You were focused on me; I was comfortable in You reverting back to my original abductor. And then I hated myself for it. The emotions surged out of the darkness in me before I could identify or understand them. I was thinking foreign, traitorous thoughts before I knew they were mine. Why was I hungry for the manipulations of my captor? Why was I not simply and purely loathing You?

Something at my very base, something instinctual and buried miles below my perplexed mind, it felt imperative. My guts said follow; my animal said be necessary; my cells said earn the food; my heart said don't get left alone here in the dark.

This could be an extension of my resolve, I told myself. This could be learning what he wants and staying alive. At first, I started acting like Yours. As I crawled complacently at Your feet and poised for instruction, I told myself it was just an act. As I bowed my head to march to the bucket, I told myself I was in control here, with my choice to submit. As I basked in Your sweet aftercare, I told myself I didn't really enjoy it; it was all part of my playing my role here.

I was selling the idea of my submission, selling the appearance of belonging to You. The sale was my control, making You believe what I wanted. And the sale was what I was best at.

My mind insisted on resistance until the bitter, shaking end. Even as forced practice became familiar, even as familiar became habit. Consistently, I told myself this was an act. *Play the part right. Sell the angle. It's working. He's buying it; he's buying it all. If I can just play long enough, I can find some way out.* I repeated these things to myself in the dark no matter how submission was welling up inside me from all sides.

The more rotations of the routine that swept over us, the harder the scab on my side became. The carefully contained and medicated red began to fully recede from the surrounding flesh and disappear back under the wound. The healthy skin, by degrees, began to crawl over the edges, gradually restaking its claim in rippled scar tissue.

As the color faded and the skin changed, an itch writhed beneath. I felt it wriggling on my nerves.

Instinctively, I would let my haggard nails rake at it, but patches were too sensitive to endure it. I had to settle for tapping the bandage or shifting my body against the bars to distract from that concentrated prickle.

Once the scab toughened and became thick, I could run my fingertips over it without flinching away from the sensitivity. My nerves retreated into my flesh. I pushed my shirt aside, stroked the smooth and furrowed scab, and teased at the edges. I tugged gently until I felt the pain, then pressed the scab back down. I traced the edges, imagining the diamond shape in my mind, marveling at how straight the edges could be.

Each night, it was harder to separate the edge from my healthy skin. Each night, the perimeter receded. Gradually, I felt more and more flesh. It was deep and marbled, smooth and hairless—a deviation from the untouched surroundings. I could trail my fingertip along the healthy skin until it dropped off onto the scar. The new skin was both muted and extra sensitive.

I was able to examine my developing scar under the light each time You spread me out onto my vacation on the mat as You cleaned and redressed me. Each time I was allowed to stretch out, I also noticed my body withering away around me. I never had an excess of weight, but it was still managing to fade. My skin was loose from the supple flesh disappearing too quickly.

When I lay on my side, my top hip and set of ribs rose out of my flesh, standing stark out of pulled skin. There was no longer a comforting layer to disguise my skeleton. My skin was slack and sort of pooled beside my body on the mat. It was fascinating and grotesque at the same time, my body so unfamiliar and alien to me. There was no mirror or reflective surface in my pit. I was wrapped up in a tight ball in my cage with no room to examine anything. The only time I could look at my own body was outside the cage, where I was often too distracted to consider it.

As I moved my limbs in the harsh light, I could see the tendons and wasted muscles shifting beneath my graying skin. I could see the roadmap of my veins so deprived of the sunlight. I was only relieved that I could not see the current state of my face. It was hard enough to face the stranger in the parts of my body I could see.

Each day, I recognized myself a little less—mentally and physically.

Once the pain had diminished and the bandage was no longer necessary, I scarcely thought about the injury. I tried to blot the entire incident out of my memory. It was easier that way. I found life more amiable when You were my caretaker, when I didn't remember the meticulous way You extracted my flesh. When my eyes did fall on the wretched diamond shape, I felt my chest tighten and my breathing quicken. I would immediately avert my eyes and shove the rising memories deeper into my darkness.

If I measured time by how long it took that diamond of flesh to fully grow back, we had existed in this healing holding pattern for months.

Surely, my life on the outside had forgotten all about me by now. No one would have known what happened to me, but they would have given up by now. Hope would have faded a little day by day, and so many days had passed now. Lei had to figure I was dead or gone forever, which maybe I was. Cops would have stopped searching, brushed me into a colder file. Work would have passed my files off to other associates, given someone else my promotion. Probably fucking Denise.

I was gone, completely gone. It was all lost, and all I had left was this small, concrete box.

I ran my hand over the scar, alone in the dark. The slick skin somehow alternated in sensitivity and numbness. The nerves tentatively stretched into the freshly grown flesh as the cells labored to reproduce the original—as closely as possible. It would never be my hip again, not really. This swatch of regrowth was Your skin, Your permanent claim to my body.

16

Then the fateful day came when I was healed enough. Lessons could resume.

It had been so long I had almost forgotten the pain, almost forgotten my purpose here.

There was no lazily outstretched mat waiting for me anymore; there was only the cold blank slate of the concrete. You no longer held alcohol and gauze; You were once again selecting from Your tools mounted on the wall. I had stopped looking at them once the pain stopped; how could they not have been a constant reminder that I would only end up back here, that all roads in this tiny box led back here?

My heart dropped in my chest when I crawled out from my cage to the empty floor and to You standing beside the door empty-handed. If Your face ever changed, the caretaker I had been quietly basking in had drained from it. Your limbs no longer moved with the soft fluidity of nurture; they were rigid to a different purpose once more.

I did not know my heart could be broken by one I did not love, by one who stripped me from my life.

I felt my legs wobble beneath me and crouched down, wrapping my arms around my knees. I knew You would instruct me; I knew I would only have to follow. Until then, I only wanted to hold myself in tragic wait. I wanted to quickly mourn the passing of my brief vacation.

You reached down and guided my chin until I was squinting up at You under that swinging bulb. I tried to read Your face in the harsh shadows the light carved in it. It was futile. You were more steeled again, rejuvenated by returning to Your work. Maybe it was a smile hiding behind those thin, pursed lips. Maybe it was a twinkle reflecting on the edge of Your eyeball.

Maybe I was imagining it in my fear.

You continued to tug at my chin until I reluctantly stood to follow the gesture. You took me by the shoulders and turned me around to face the blank wall. Then You lifted my arms and slid Your gloved hands down them until You extended them out and pressed them into the wall. I could feel the rough paint abrading my neglected palms.

When You flattened my hand against the wall, You looked back at me and pressed Your hand on top of them firmly. *Keep your hands here.* I nodded shakily as tears started to well behind my eyes. From then, I could only hear You. I did not dare turn my head, crane my neck trying to see what was coming.

I heard the subtle tinkling and scraping as You ran Your fingers over the instruments. The chain clanked against the concrete. The straps slapped against each other. All harsh and unforgiving materials brushing against more harsh and unforgiving surfaces. With each noise, my body tightened. I felt my skin tense fearfully, a conditioned response.

This is what You wanted.

Your hand made a selection. Your footsteps marched up behind me. I felt them move closer in the imagined vibrations of the floor. I flinched as I felt You slide my shirt up to expose the skin of my back, yet I no longer foolishly feared rape. I knew You desired something entirely different of my flesh. I felt myself contract as I tried to curl all parts of me as close as possible, without breaking Your positioning. If I clenched enough, I could protect myself a little.

The implement split my back in a sharp line of pain. I gasped at the vividness of it, the way I could feel the sensation clean through my torso to the other side. My belly dropped as my back fled the strike, but I did not dare shift my hands. I kept them planted, though wriggling, in the impressions they had left in the dust. My fingertips dug desperately into the concrete until the tips and knuckles turned white.

I peeled my eyes back open and breathed harshly against my own body, trying to dispel the shrieking of my nerves. You were waiting for me to recover. I could hear You tapping it against the palm of Your glove methodically. A whip maybe. Perhaps a switch. I felt the shock waves spread and finally flatten over my body, leaving all my skin buzzing, leaving goose bumps trailing in strange patterns.

Then I steeled myself for the next.

You took it easy on me, considering. Perhaps You did not want to destroy me after I had grown so complacent. I could not think straight to discern Your design with the pain throbbing into my brain, demanding my constant attention. I had forgotten how primal and consuming it was, the way I completely lost myself in it.

I would forget that many times.

You divided my back no more than five times. Then I heard the instrument find its home back on the wall. I still did not move, tensing my fingers against their place on the wall, feeling the texture of the cracks and rough paint. I could feel the blood slowly trickling down the curvature of my spine. It was light and thin, so I knew the wounds were not deep. You had just opened the sensitive surface.

You left me standing there, awkwardly, wallowing in the lesson, for a long moment. My anger toward You burrowed deep through me. I felt it burning in my belly, a deep, radiating heat. You had constructed the comfort for me to fall from deliberately. You had broken me down and built me back up just to be able to devastate me once more.

This was a game to You.

I was a game to You.

You were a sick fucking bastard.

Yet I remained there, immobile, seething in my own skin. I heard You exit the room and return. Then I heard the familiar flop of the mat on the floor. My heart jumped back at out my stomach; my ears perked. I wanted to turn around and look, for I was surely imagining it.

You stepped around me, and by the wrists, You guided my hands away from the wall. I looked tentatively into Your eyes for just a second and glimpsed something softer. The rigidity had fallen from Your form as You led me to the mat and directed me to my belly. Sheepishly, I spread myself flat and vulnerable and folded my arms under my head.

You knelt down beside me. The unscrewing of the lid, the slosh of the alcohol, the bite on my skin. I nuzzled against my own forearms as You cleaned and dressed me. As the pain faded, so did the veracity of the memory. Once the vice released my nerves, my mind instantly strove to abolish the evidence. Like I always heard it was like in childbirth.

You forget how much it hurts.

Your swipes along my wounds painted the pattern in my mind. They were long and thin strokes, barely intersecting. You had drawn near parallel cuts down my once plain and unadorned back. I imagined the bright red lines through my pale skin, the flesh surrounding them angry with sympathy, the swelling rising as the injuries sunk in.

When You finished applying the bandages, You pulled me back up to my feet. You stood me against the same wall. You pressed my hands. You retrieved the mat and left the room once more.

Again, You did not bolt the door. Again, I made no effort to lunge for it.

I waited at my place on the wall. You returned with a chair in one hand and an indistinguishable handful of something in the other.

Where is this going? Aren't I supposed to go back into my cage? Aren't we done?

You placed the chair in the center of the space in the room, adjacent to my cage, parallel to the wall of tools. And I instantly knew to sit in it. Though utterly bewildered, I did as I knew You wanted. I stepped forward with cautious steps, checking Your approval each time I dropped the sole of my foot to the concrete. You simply stood still and waited for my compliance.

It felt foreign to sit in a chair. My body no longer knew how to fold into perpendicular angles. I wanted to lay out flat on my mat. I wanted to live on that mat. I didn't feel like any good could come from this awkward intruder in my cell, this inappropriate furniture forced in.

As You moved around the chair and in front of me, I could discern You were holding a handful of straps. My chest coiled tighter. First, You secured my ankles to the legs of the chair, gently but firmly tightening each strap until motion was denied. You extended each of my arms along the back of the chair until You could bind them to the posts that met the seat.

You raised one more strap in front of my face. It was divided in the center by a large, red ball. I rolled my lips into my mouth and pressed my teeth down at the sight of it. I wanted to turn my head away, but I didn't dare. You held it in front of my mouth for a second. Then I heard You let a warning breath out of Your nose, and I dropped my jaw.

You gently seated the ball between my lips and buckled the strap behind my head. I hated the full sensation in my mouth. I detested being forced to breathe through my nose.

You placed Your hand softly on the top of my head and leaned toward my face. Eye to eye, You brought a finger across Your lips. Not a sound.

Then You silenced the light and stepped out of the room, leaving the door ajar just enough to let a sliver carve the dark wall.

You left me awkwardly situated alone in the dark so long that I began to nod off. It was amazing the positions I could sleep in at this point. But then the sound pulled me back from the edge of consciousness.

It was a woman's voice.

My heart seized in my chest, frozen between beats. I could not make out the words, but it was a woman talking just behind and beyond my door.

Holy shit, are You luring in another one? Am I about to share my cell with another captive?

I couldn't breathe, even above the gag. I tried to thrash silently on the increasingly uncomfortable chair. My heart had started pounding so hard I could see it in the edges of the dark.

She was continuing to talk, but I never heard You. I strained to the limits of my hearing, willing my eardrums to stretch out past the door that hid me. You either did not speak or did not speak audibly for me.

No no no no. God no. Not another one.

I did not want another woman in here with me. The thought of company was actually upsetting to me. At first, I was not sure why. I only knew the thought was blaring through my mind. I did not want another woman suffering the way I was suffering, yet I did not want You to supplement me, to replace me. The idea of sharing Your attention amplified my anxiety. Competition could undo any progress I had made in my manipulation, any strides I had accomplished toward my eventual freedom.

I worked alone.

I willed her to run. I pleaded for her to flee. I screamed silently in my mind, as if she could hear me.

But I did not make a sound. As I was told.

There were tears on my cheeks. I could feel my nose running down over the ball gag. I tried to calm myself quietly so I did not choke on my sobs. I forced the quivering breaths through my nose until my body stopped shaking. I could not save her. And I could not stop listening.

Then her sounds changed. The words I could not articulate faded out. At first, I thought it was the muffled sounds of pain, but as they built, I knew they were not. My body knew those sounds. I felt my skin involuntarily flush as my blood redirected toward my center. I felt my sensual nerves awaken. Her noises climbed and progressed until climax.

She was having an orgasm. I realized that my prison was in Your closet, that Your bedroom was always there on the other side of my door. You slept on the other side of the wall with me locked in here.

What the fuck!

Why does he want me to hear this? Why is he putting on this show? Is he still planning to shove her into this cell after he's done with her?

I detested my arousal, but I could not resist those sounds of a woman. I despised the way it resurrected Lei in my mind. The way she bit her lip and twisted a ball of the sheets into her fist when she came. The way I had to wrap my hands around her hips to keep her from fleeing the climax.

Goddamn him.

Was this just another form of torture? Was her pleasure just a device to remind me of what I had lost, what I would never regain in this prison?

How could You do this to me directly after splitting my back? You hadn't even given me recovery this time.

You did it to her again and again, until I could scarcely bare it. I tried to escape into my mind, but all avenues led to Lei writhing beneath me, which only amplified my anguish. When the sounds finally relented, I dove off the edge into the oblivion of a very unpleasant sleep.

17

I woke up when the light spilled across my face as You opened the door. I snapped my wrenched neck up to see if You were dragging the woman behind You.

You stood in the doorframe alone. The room behind You was silent.

I assumed I would have heard her dying; I assumed You used her and let her leave. With relief dripping over my brain, I was able to take note of the fierce aches in my body. My neck kinked violently after hours of my head dangling unsupported in the weight of my sleep. My low back tightened against the rigid seat and the spine still stacked crookedly on top of it. My hips had relented and fallen asleep sometime in the night.

You were smiling openly, but with closed lips, when You leaned down to release my arms and legs.

What is he trying to show me? What is this supposed to prove?

Once the mild euphoria dissipated through my body, I felt my rage again. I was so fully and completely mad at You. Furious that You brought back the pain, disappointed that You tainted my one respite in aftercare, livid that You had set up me up to listen to You have sex all night.

Did it get You off to know I could hear You? Was that how You were going to steal sexuality from me?

Maybe You weren't different. Maybe You were just the deviant I had feared You were.

I did not know how I was feeling. My emotions were a tumultuous storm thrashing under my heart. I did not know why I cared, why I was so hurt by this new offense. They were just sounds. What were sounds in the scheme of this place? I could not have actually preferred Your attention focused on me instead.

Did You just want to show me You were a man, with normal desires and a normal life outside these walls?

I was too upset to rationalize Your motives and behaviors. I had to stretch my logic and analytical mind to its limits to wrap around Your world, and it was drowning in that sea under my chest.

You were relaxed, unfocused, immune to the anger radiating from my tensed muscles and sideways glances. Maybe You were remembering her, basking in flashes of the night before the way I remembered doing every time with Lei.

That was it. That was why I was a mess.

Sex led to Lei in my primal wiring. Your sex summoned her back to my mind, resuscitated that excruciating longing for her.

And if You did that deliberately, it was far more sadistic than any strike across my skin.

You faced me toward the bucket then turned Your back to permit me partial privacy. When I was done, I crawled past You and into my cage. I never thought I would welcome the feeling of that meager blanket. I never imagined missing my confined quarters, but curling up tightly on my side, feeling those bars against my hip, made my body feel normal. It was almost starting to feel like home.

I was happy for the darkness. I was glad to be left alone in my cell. You returned and deposited my plate of food, but I left it untouched beside my feet. I did not want to do anything but lie here exactly how I had fantasized while in that chair. I wanted to sleep until I forgot all the feelings seething inside me.

And I did sleep. Most of the day. A heavy, feverish sleep that had me plunging in and out of deep pools of twisted dreams. I could not wrap the fingers of my perception around the scenes. I was only left floating among the fragments when I washed up in my cage before slipping under once more.

Wrapping my fingers into Lei's woven bracelets. The sound of a switch dragging along the bars of my cage.

McAllister's pants pluming wet and pungent against my face as I napped on the couch.

The swatch of my bloody flesh spread out over an instrument tray.

Swirling, writhing images flirting with my consciousness from the depths of my subconscious.

I would wallow in them happily, rolling in the heavy blanket on my mind, over dealing with the reality that waited for me between the concrete walls.

You released me to my bucket again, brought me another plate I chose not to eat. I knew the lesson was coming, but I decided not to care.

This time, I was making a new choice. I was no longer resolving to submit, to fake obedience in order to sell You. Fuck that. Tonight, defiance was alive in my brain. Tonight, I had no long-term goal; I only wanted to indulge my rage and my disdain. Whatever the price might prove to be, I needed this small rebellion.

Maybe You would just kill me. Maybe You would just finally end it. And maybe that would be for the best. I had spent enough nights sweetly courting Death, begging for him to just take me and make the pain stop.

You came in to teach me. I did not look up when You crouched down to unlock the cage. I heard the whine of the cage door and rolled over to acknowledge You then turned my back to You and closed my eyes. You walked briskly to the wall of tools then returned and rapped on the cage bars with the switch. I ignored You.

If I couldn't escape You, maybe I could convince You to kill me. Fight sure hadn't inspired homicide in You. Quite the opposite. Maybe indifference would push You far enough.

You hit the switch against the bars again, harder. I could hear Your impatience in the increasing strength in the strikes. By this time, I could hear Your voice in Your actions and mannerisms, like I could read Your mind. You stood there, inflating from cold to rage, letting Your thoughts radiate over me. I lay unaffected. This would be my insubordination.

Fuck compliance. Fuck surviving. It was time for rebellion.

I knew when I could hear You release a breath and turn around, it was going to be bad.

I knew when I heard the metal of the chain links clinking together, we were going to explore a new dimension of education.

The cold links bit my skin as You wrapped the chain around my ankle. Then I felt the tension tighten; the links tore into me, pushed until they compressed my nerves and my blood flow, as You ripped me out of my cage by my ankle. My hip collided with and scraped over the frame of the cage door; the cement crashed against my body as I stuttered along it.

I think I howled out in both surprise and pain. Nerves all over my body were firing through the panic. But my mind screamed fuck you just the same. I would not fight, and I would not wilt. I would be nothing.

I did not cradle my aching points or curl up and cower. I lay on the gray floor like a corpse, staring blankly at the dusty floor, feeling my own breath bounce back into my face.

You snatched me by the hair and dragged me up to my feet. I felt every follicle in Your grasp scream and pull, but I steeled my jaw and forced myself to not make a sound this time. No sound, no reaction. I kept my limbs limp and uncooperative despite the adrenaline throbbing through my system. My base self wanted to fight or wanted to submit; I had to consciously suppress myself into this outward seeming apathy.

Rage was in the force of Your touch but not in Your pace. You kept to Your methodical and meticulous practices. You looped the chain eloquently around me. I felt the cold length coil around my arms then my torso then my legs in unfamiliar patterns. Finally, You brought it around my throat, a sensation that made my heart pause, before guiding it up around the mounted hook. The pressure was laced over and back and between until I was half suspended upright and terribly uncomfortable.

My arms were lashed unnaturally behind me, wrapped against each other until I could feel the wretched stretch tearing across my pectorals, digging deep into the tendons across my shoulders. My chest felt splayed by the contortion.

My legs were tangled awkwardly, keeping every joint engaged and every muscle struggling to support my knotted position. My feet quivered weakly, unable to sustain my weight, unable to release the pose. I could feel the acid building and pooling in my thighs; I could hear the chain grumbling as they quivered relentlessly.

The binding kept my spine rigid. The slightest slouch brought the links deeper into my throat and restricted my breathing. I felt the tension mounting between each disk, the ache that crept into the surrounding muscles and curled around my ribs. My shoulders began to turn in on themselves, the rigidity spreading its throbbing fingers up into my neck and the base of my skull, which now seemed so impossibly heavy.

There were too many points of pain for my brain to choose from, rolled onto my toes, half-squatting, chain gently pressing against my throat, arms held useless behind me.

Those first hours were sheer torture. My mind was simply a blur; I could scarcely distinguish a sensation and had lost all coherent ability to form thoughts. Words and sounds screamed through my head, but I could barely tell if there were in my brain or in the room around me. My muscles felt like they were ripping; my skeleton felt like it was fracturing. Every single nerve shrieked at full volume.

Enough pressure and time finally brought the sensation of pins and needles to my extremities. Then they slowly began to vanish from my awareness. My nerves gradually surrendered, and I went numb. I do not believe the pain stopped; I only think my perception of it changed. After so long, after so much, out of survival, my brain elected to begin shutting it out, begin shutting down. My body was warped so uncomfortably that my mind could only hear its incessant pleas to make it fucking stop.

You brought that fucking chair back into the room, a wooden foreigner in my country of cement and metal. You placed it directly in front of me and sat, staring me calmly dead in the face. Somehow, Your eyes on me made it all the more painful and uncomfortable. Something in the way You could just watch me suffer, the way it did not register on Your face at all. I could not bear to look into Your dead eyes, yet You had me so contorted that it was the only natural position for my gaze.

Everything planned, down the smallest and most vivid detail.

You sat in symmetry. Your feet were flat on the floor, legs in perfect angles above them. You put each hand on each knee. Your shoulders were rolled down and relaxed, making Your neck look all the longer. Your jaw cut another straight line into Your neck as Your placid face simply observed me. You rested unaffected as I twitched and writhed against the chain, as I whimpered and quietly let the tears roll down my face.

Then amidst the turmoil, my mind found a single point of clarity, a momentary oasis in the storm of my anguish.

I woke up in the hospital in a paralytic haze. The weight of the anesthesia crushed my awareness and muddled my senses. The lights seemed blindingly bright above me. I squinted against them and found it difficult to wrestle my eyes back open again. My mouth felt completely parched, tongue sticking to the roof and my cheeks. I tried to swallow, to solicit any saliva, yet my throat ached, as if the tube was still stretching against it.

Lei's hand found mine as I floundered in my consciousness. The sensation of her skin, the familiar shape of her fingers grounded me back in the moment, even as my mind continued to swim.

"It's okay, baby," she whispered near my ear. "It's over. Just rest now. I'm right here."

I let my eyes fall shut again as a lazy smile played on my lips at her words. I tuned out the stimuli of the unfamiliar hospital room and allowed myself to scan my own body. As my evaluation moved down my torso, I felt nothing. A crushing feeling of emptiness registered under my abdomen, where my womb used to be. I had never considered the thing much before, aside from when it warped against me monthly, yet I found myself experiencing its void in a way I did not anticipate.

I shifted my hips, breathed deep into my belly, tightened my muscles into a Kegel. Nothing. It all felt like a gaping, heavy nothing.

I felt tears burning at the edges of my eyes when I opened them again. Lei had retracted her hand without my noticing. Instead, I was greeted by a foreign figure in hospital scrubs. A nurse, maybe an orderly. I knew nothing of hospital stratification.

He leaned over his cart and very carefully sorted through medication, comparing what he lifted to his face with a chart held in his other hand. I noticed his hair first, dark, precisely combed to leave a rigid part down his scalp.

Lei walked back into the room, a soda can cupped in her hand. She smiled and spoke softly to the man. He looked down as he replied into the clipboard.

He finally seemed satisfied at the contents in the small paper cup and walked very deliberately toward me. His steps were unnaturally slow, and something about his mere presence seemed to beckon anxiety deep inside my chest, somewhere adjacent to my new emptiness. As he placed the cup in my hand, he met my eyes for just a second. They were dark, seemingly black, and startlingly cold.

It was You.

I could hear the chain clinking against itself and dragging against the floor. I could hear my own cries and whines and my own heartbeat throbbing in my ears and against every link of the chain and in every contorted joint and twisted skin. I could hear Your gentle breathing, creating rhythm against the furious chaos enveloping me. Seconds banged out eternities as I struggled just to breathe, to go anywhere but here.

I could still feel that hospital bed at the edges of my brain. The first glimpse of You mocked me and how long it took to fish it out of the tangles in my head. The moment had been locked in there all along, hazed over and tucked away. You had seen me then. For some reason, You had selected me then.

That was over three years ago.

I did not want to think about it; maybe I had been blocking it out all this time. I tried to conjure any other memory. I scraped against my brain, raked my nails over the matter desperately trying to dig out one pleasant moment. Yet the soil was now barren. There was only You staring back at me. I cried out from my deepest gut at the last mourning of the former me.

I felt something collapse in my heart, in my soul. I felt something deep within me break.

This was the single moment when I became Yours, the one instance where I fully and completely crossed that line.

Then the epiphany hit me. Harder than any realization in my life. More poignant than when I articulated I had no interest in lying with any man, when thought finally articulated what my soul always knew. I didn't want to accept it; some fragment of me tried to resist it, yet it rose slowly and thickly in my brain just the same. I felt the honesty in it resonate through my bones like a tuning fork.

I had no control; I never did. My choices were nothing more than a creature comfort, nothing real about them.

This was Your world, and I was Yours.

You saw the change in me. My body went limp; my sounds were silenced. You were more inside my head than I was able to read Your will. You were inside my very flesh, knew me better than I ever hoped to know myself. You stood slowly with a phantom of a smile at the edges of Your mouth. You removed the intruding chair and returned to me, slowly uncoiling me from the chain.

Blood flushed through my system unrestricted, pounded through my temples, flooded my brain. I felt myself wobble, nearly drunk on it, intoxicated at the relief. That solace lined the vivid pain as pins and needles assaulted my nerves, as my body remembered the parts it had been striving to ignore through the ordeal. I tingled from my hair to my toenails.

It was finally over. I had survived this test. All the screaming in my flesh stopped, and the world was suddenly very quiet. I closed my eyes to absorb the recession of my pain.

With the chain removed, You supported my body, guiding me down to a position I could sustain on my own, collapsed into a pile on the concrete with my head rolling around like a newborn. My eyes were still lazily closed when I heard the latex snap. You were removing Your gloves.

Then You touched me. No implement or tool, no glove between us. Your skin came into contact with mine. The feeling of Your warm, smooth hand on my neck was electric. It shocked my nerves the way no touch had before. Not even her sweet touch. She used to make me cum until the edge of the world started to blur. This was different. It had been so long since I felt the heat of flesh. My skin had forgotten what anything but cold and wet and metal felt like. To have that one sensation of humanity against my nerves snapped me out of my swirling inner torment and brought me a clarity of purpose. A gentle touch from You, Your smallest affection was all I craved, became all I sought to obtain.

With Your warm hand on my neck, You moved me to sit in front of You. You knelt behind me. I did not know what to expect, but after enduring such a torturous stress position for so long, I didn't much give a shit. I let my eyes stay closed as I simply waited.

You brushed my hair. Such a surprisingly affectionate gesture that I flinched. I didn't even know where the brush came from, if it had been hiding in my cell all along. You lay bristles to my scalp. I remained frozen, mouth agape, arms suspended in disbelief as You put one hand to my shoulder to indicate I should stay and pulled the brush down through the strands. Each stroke hypnotized me. With each pass, my muscles released, and I melted into a puddle in front of You.

18

Once I yielded, once I both truly became Yours and accepted it, it became a different imprisonment. I simply stopped. Stopped fighting. Stopped trying. Stopped missing. Stopped wanting. Stopped feeling. Stopped thinking. Stopped plotting. Stopped dreaming.

I stopped, and the world stopped turning. Life stopped existing outside of my room. I surrendered to You and let You resuscitate me into this new existence. I didn't have to try; I only had to follow.

Everything gradually just eroded within me. Not unlike the body that contained it. As my body wasted and sagged, my memories wilted, faded, reduced to only disjointed fragments. My thoughts devolved and became more simplistic and primal.

I used to miss them all—Lei, McAllister, my dead mother, even Julie—when my ego still infected me. I used to lie on my side in my cage and stare into the dark. I let memory swell over me until I was in our bed. As I pressed my hand against the cold bars, I felt the soft warmth of her bare shoulder. I saw the corner of her mouth fall open as she snored softly. Her bangs stuck to her forehead. I would reach up and brush them aside, as I always did while she was sleeping. It used to be thoughts of her that kept me alive, dreams of seeing her again, feeling her body line up in perfect symmetry with mine as she clung to me for the first time.

I tried to cleave to her, fight the dying of the light inside me. I shouldn't be able to forget her; I shouldn't be able to forsake that life. Yet survival made such a compelling argument. Sacrifice it all to keep having anything. I learned to forget her. The light drained out of my memories, and only the shadow of us lying together remained, dead and unmoving.

My focus shifted. You were the life in my world. You were the only thing that pulled me from the sludge of what remained inside my head and parted the heavy dark solitude. You were it.

Each time You cleaned my wound or placed the plate beside me was a reminder that You were my life; You were what kept me alive. Each trial enlightened me to the poison that she was, deceiving me into believing choice existed. She let me believe that I wanted her, that I was capable of and allowed to want. But You opened my eyes. With the taste of blood in my mouth, I was born into Your truth. The only truth. Your sweet slavery set me free. Free of my pointless striving, free of my love for her, free of dreams of a life now gone. A peace only the possessed can know.

Shrieks, screams, curses became whimpers before fading into compliance. My posturing wilted, shoulders dropping from defiance to hunger and exhaustion to slumped submission. First, You disciplined me for resistance, then for apathy, then as affection.

The morning after You tangled me in the chain and left me hanging until I finally and completely broke, You were different, victorious maybe. Not the way You were after teaching me, not the way You were after the night with the other woman. This was new, calmer, infectious.

You took my hand as You guided me out of my cage. You were no longer wearing gloves. I felt the electricity and humanity in Your skin, and it sustained me.

I trusted You now. I knew the right answer was just to follow, to be Yours.

You stood me gently beside my cage then took a step back. You retrieved a small, black digital camera from Your pocket and held it out in front of You. The display screen splashed colors against Your face. The device looked near foreign to me now, and I shrunk from it. I felt a deep and forgotten pang of vanity, of shame and disgust at my now gruesome form.

I did not want to be immortalized like this.

You looked at me, almost reassuring me, then pressed the shutter. I flinched against the harsh flash. You checked the image on the screen then returned the camera to Your pocket.

You stepped out of the room, leaving the door not just unlatched by wide open. I took a small step forward and leaned, craning my neck to see Your room on the other side. I could make out a large, dark wooden dresser with heavy, ominous hardware gleaming in the center of each drawer. Before I could take another step, You returned.

You had a book folded in Your arms. It was large and thick, the way I remembered traditional photo albums from my childhood. The ones with plastic over the pictures. My mother would cradle me in her lap as she pointed to each face, making me recite relatives I saw only twice a year.

That's your daddy, she would say to the earliest pictures. I never would identify him when she pointed to his face.

You turned the book over in Your hands then extended Your arms and offered it to me. I turned my head and looked at You quizzically. Then, tentatively, I reached out and grasped it. The book had some weight to it, and the cover felt thick against my fingers. It dropped into my arms, and I slowly crouched to sitting as I faced it toward me.

The cover was plain, a dark-brown fake leather with gold lines scrolled along the edges. I curled my legs under me and brought my elbows close against my body as I let my fingertips rest on the edges of the book. The pages were limp, soft, and worn. Your thumbs had played through them many times, compulsively even, habitually even. Your touch was on this book.

I felt the cold concrete pressing into my sit bones.

My shoulders slumped as the book enticed my curiosity simply by sitting in my lap. My heart was fluttering in my chest. I had no idea what to expect. Something comforting, something horrific. There could be anything under this cover, and in this place, that was terrifying. My fingers shook a little as I looked up at You. You simply waited.

I cast my eyes back down and slowly cracked the cover. There was one picture on the first page. As my eyes cautiously brought it into focus, I realized it was my cell. My cage and the concrete walls were in the background. An emaciated woman hunched beside the cage, right where I now sat. She cowered fearfully and squinted at the camera out of the corner of her eye, wrapping her arms protectively around herself.

My heart started beating faster, and I felt my breathing falter.

I twitched my fingers to the corner and turned the page. The next page was the same woman in the same cell. She was no longer standing. Her body was collapsed on the floor unnaturally, limbs turned in awkward directions. Her neck was twisted and discolored, and her head fell at an angle that betrayed her demise.

Now I could hear my heart in my ears. It throbbed in my peripherals. My vision was pulsating nauseatingly.

The next page was a new woman, equally starved, equally dressed, positioned beside our cage. She was not fearful though; she had defiance and hatred painted in the thin angles of her face. She did not hunch; she stood tall and rebellious with her shoulders high and one hand on a hip.

I did not want to turn the page. I knew what was next.

She was in pieces. Her insubordination had clearly upset You, and she had clearly paid for it. I cringed away from it and fled to the next page.

Four more girls followed them, all variations on the original two. All failures.

I was number seven.

I turned to the next page, and it was blank. This was my page. This was where You would place the picture You had just snapped. And the blank page that followed it would decide my fate. It would define my success or document my failure.

You were showing me Your history. You were showing me how much You had worked to get here, how much had preceded me. This was the fruit of Your mind for however many years.

"It was you." I breathed. I finally mustered up enough courage to speak it. "It was you in that hospital, when I had my hysterectomy."

You did not say anything. Instead, You crouched down and gathered up the book, closing the cover and turning it into Your chest. As You cradled Your pictorial history, Your visual track record, You looked down. It was a rare instance for You to cast Your eyes down when not to a task. A memory sparked over my brain. It was the same way You looked down in my hospital room when Lei had spoken to You.

You're going to take good care of my girl, aren't you?

"It was you," I said again with certainty.

Somehow knowing, somehow connecting the dots in my mind flooded a heavy calm through my veins. You had selected me years in advance. You had watched me, chosen me. This was not some random act of violence. Maybe that shouldn't have made me feel better, yet it consoled me. It was a logic that made this whole scenario make some semblance of sense to me.

It also meant You had chosen me for a reason.

"You chose me then," I said. "Why? Why me? Why did you watch me for so long?"

I don't know why I asked the questions; I knew You would not speak, would not answer me. They had been knocking around in my brain for however many days had passed black over me in this box. I couldn't not ask them at this point.

Your face spoke volumes to me. Still holding the book against Your chest, You looked back up and into my eyes. The eye contact was electric; I felt it shoot down my entire spine. The muscles around Your eyes slackened, lifting Your eyebrows so slightly.

Your jaw released, allowing Your lips to relax and not appear so thin and tight. Your expression was as plain and simple as what it meant.

You are mine.

For whatever reason, You decided that then, as I wallowed overmedicated in that hospital bed, bidding farewell to my primal, biological femininity. Perhaps You were seduced by me in that state, a state not all that different from the one into which You broke me down. Weak and physically broken, mentally longing for pieces of me that were lost.

What a poetic little circle You created with me.

You knelt down in front of me, reached out, and tucked the hair behind my ear.

You are mine.

And I was Yours. It was no longer an act or a game or a manipulation. I looked up at You from the fucking bottom, from the base of submission and acceptance. The breakdown was behind us; the fight was worn out of me. Now Your real work could begin.

We embarked into our real routine. You provided just enough food to silence my belly, just enough water to lubricate my throat. You taught me every day. You were my savior from gluttony and compliance. You were right; I looked better this thin. Slender, frail, heroin chic. You knew how much I needed and how much I deserved. I never could appreciate the beauty of my own skeleton before. The innate sexiness of the contour of my protruding ribs, the sharp curve of my hip. I never knew I was hiding all this beneath such gluttonous flesh.

The more I withered, the more I became what You wanted. Like unearthing a fossil, You were dusting away my version of me to reveal the skeletal structure of Your rendering.

Two meager meals, two evacuations, then my lesson. I used to dread it. As my mind discerned the pattern in the chaos of captivity, I would start trembling as the hours marched me closer. I could feel the impending pain hovering above me, thickening the air. I imagined You designed this torturous waiting period. I could see You grinning slyly as You knew I was writhing in anticipation on the other side of the door.

At first, I was convinced You must hate me. I had to be a fleshy outlet of anger, loathing, pure evil. How could anyone do this to another human being? Yet, as the shock wore off, as the trauma became my reality, when it was long enough for me to truly take a perspective on it, Your true purpose began to reveal itself to me. Slowly teasing me with glimpses at enlightenment, my own mind coyly playing with me. But it became clear to me.

I started to really only live when You occupied my cold, small space with me. Though a flicker of me did persist in solitude. A soft and muted piece of me hobbled through those waits for You. The wide imaginative expanse of my mind contracted from the whole world of perception and far reaches of fantasy, folded and curled up inside only these walls. There was no reason to let myself linger in that forgotten outside world. Instead, I strove to keep myself here, to be just for You. However, as lifeless and catatonic as my bones hibernated in the quiet hours, I could not kill the extent of my mind. I could not confine it only in my cage.

I only permitted myself a smile when I was alone. I imagined my now thin lips stretching back to reveal neglected teeth. The skin lifted and pulled in forgotten patterns. My mouth pointed to sunken cheeks and tortured eyes. In my mind, I did not recognize myself. I did not look like the woman I left in the mirror; I had been reshaped to Your vision. A corpse to the world. Your corpses did not smile, but alone in the dark, I let my enslaved joy betray Your masterpiece. A smile was my quiet and last rebellion, yet it was still for You.

Sometimes I sang to myself, in the dark, in the quiet, when I knew You had left. After Your shadow had abandoned my sliver of light long enough, I allowed my cracked lips to part and my voice to scratch out old tunes. Something simple and basic, embedded in the ruins of my mind.

Twinkle, twinkle.

Making sound felt foreign, as if another was pulling my vocal cords.

Little star.

She was so weak and beaten, gasping between verses and so different from the one who thrived within my head.

How I wonder.

I let those songs my mother used to sing to me rasp out of my throat and tried not to feel her cuddle me tightly against her chest in the dim of my nightlight, feeling her warm, comforting arms around me and her voice vibrating against my ear.

What you are.

The child rhymes dangled in the darkness momentarily before colliding with the prison walls and turning to more dust.

Yet night by night, these dreams faded, slowly shriveled up without the light. Hope became a memory and then a figment. Each lesson only infected me with doubt. The more You scribed Your word into my flesh with welts and cuts, the more it began to seem true. The more I starved in every way possible, the more I no longer needed it.

Eventually, I could no longer fathom what that rush of freedom would feel like. The idea of finding myself outside of my dark room would waft around my mind like a wayward leaf in the wind. I would struggle to mentally capture it, pull it down, and embrace it once more. I tried to still want it, still believe it could happen, but it all just faded into the dark. It just dissipated against the concrete.

After that, I no longer lusted over it. Then I feared the idea itself. How could I survive in the light again? How could I look them in the face, let them see me? What would I even do out there? Lei would look at my disgusting, shriveled body, and a grimace of shock and disgust would distort her beautiful face. My coworkers would look at me with my sunken eyes and loose-fitting skirt suit and see only weakness; they would have advantageous pity in their eyes, and their whispers from the water cooler would be deafening. I would not remember how to sleep in the soft spacious spread of a bed. I would wake up in a ball on the floor or tucked inside McAllister's crate because it would feel safe and familiar.

I wouldn't be human again, couldn't be. I could never be anywhere but here again. Any place my body could run, my mind would still be right here, safely in Your cage.

Submission had happened gradually, by degrees, like itching down into a scalding bath. It crept up the back of my mind and spread itself through me in such a quiet accident, I scarcely noticed until I was deeply entwined in its tentacles. It was just one random day when I lay bruised and bleeding at the bottom of my cage. I felt it slip into me. Slow. Just that one innocuous little thought.

Just do what he wants.

That one thought, my foolish little resolve had been the first crack that would eventually shatter me. It was all over in that one instant; it just took me this long to accept it.

I saw it now. When You found me, I was a fool. Delusions of self-importance filled my head. Of course I mattered; I was pulling down six figures with full benefits, which included health insurance with domestic partner benefits for Lei after I came out. The illusion of independence plagued my life. Of course I commanded my life; my mother reared a confident woman who powered out of her house and into the world, taking it by the balls and twisting it until she got what she wanted.

I was lost and reeling without Your sweet control. I couldn't see that I was a slave to my expectations, driven under the lash of chasing some dream birthed in a classroom daydream. I was broken until You broke my will.

Each day, I waited for the soft creak of the door. The light would spill across the concrete and crawl up the walls in twisted shadows. I would feel a twitch of exhilaration, distant like a memory. I would begin to stir behind my bars, animate from my solitary hibernation for You. You crouched down beside my cage and looked at me coolly as You turned the lock. You stayed close to the floor as You swung the door open, metal hinges whining. I emerged from the cage, crawling on stooped limbs, face upturned to receive Your signals. I squatted submissively at Your feet and stretched my arms up to You, always offering myself again.

You lightly wrapped Your fingers around my frail wrists. I closed my eyes and let my head hang back as the sensation of contact sent heat racing across my skin. I clung to that second, stretched my emaciated being out to exist in that one sensation. The warmth of those fingertips in firm command, holding me by my arms and my mind that followed them. Could You just restrain me here forever?

Then the second was gone. Your grip tightened to guide me to my feet. I wobbled on fragile legs that repeatedly forgot their purpose. My muscles quivered, trying to remember the simplicity of standing. You led me patiently, always drawing me up out of my hunched form. Time stopped again when I finally uncurled enough to stand before You, gazing cautiously up into

Your face. I breathed in that instant when I saw cold approval staring blankly back at me.

Then it was the lesson. Maybe You reminded me of the day You broke my will and suspended me in blissful agony of some new, contorted stress position. Maybe You revisited my early instruction with lashes from the strap, painting my body with welts. Maybe You let me imagine the possibilities as You meticulously cleaned and sharpened Your tools as I crouched by Your feet. Maybe You flayed a small part of my skin, allowing me a small window into my flesh. The lessons rotated in a seemingly random pattern, but I knew You had a design. I knew every torture was a step, a means, a part of crafted puzzle. I knew only that I was to follow.

In the fading echoes of my cries, as the blood dripping slowed and congealed, Your teaching sunk into my mind and into my flesh. The cold professor gave way to the caretaker. Your icy demeanor was betrayed by the traces of pride You let taint Your mannerisms. You cleaned me slowly, gently. You nursed each wound individually and fully, resting one hand upon my shoulder as the other softly swept sterile cloth over cut, contusion, or welt.

Every night after I surrendered, You brushed my hair. The gesture would mark the end of each of our days. This was our routine. You released me from my cage; You taught me; You cared for the collateral damage of Your tutelage; then You knelt me in front of You. The brush bristles grazed my scalp as You pulled them steadily from my forehead down. I felt it tickle my back as my ever-growing hair ended. You moved the brush with one hand and chased it with the other, smoothing with Your palm. I closed my eyes in a trance and only remained aware enough to hold my head exactly as You placed it.

When I heard the brush hung on the wall with the tools again, I instinctively knew to stand and face You. You looked into my eyes, actually connected with me for the briefest of instances, and ran Your hand over my hair once more. Then back into my cage. The whine of the cage door, the click of the lock, the creak of the room door, the rattle of the latch, the swell of the darkness.

19

This was my life. Every day. Until today.

Today, You are testing me.

Hours early, long before I expect You, before the rhythm of my cells know You will enter, You open the door to my room wide, letting harsh, sharp light invade. It assaults my weak pupils and seems different today, brighter. The yellow in the rays seems like an intruder; the difference makes me anxious.

I lift my heavy head from the thin blanket, prop myself up on my arm and squint up at You. Since my body started keeping track, You have never arrived early; You have never deviated from Your routine or Your plan. You move slowly and almost hesitantly but still with purpose, kneeling on the concrete beside my bars.

You take the lock in Your hand, yet it just linger there. Your fingers dangle loosely around the shape. I hear the metals shifting against each other as Your grip bobs with Your breathing. The moment freezes around us, encapsulates us awkwardly. I feel my confusion swelling around my heart, pressing against my lungs. This seems random, spontaneous even in the way You look at me through the bars. Your eyes penetrate me, peer into me, searching for something.

My Master is not spontaneous. My Master is not random. My Master does not need to search me because He already knows.

The lack of the appearance of my Master in You now might be the most frightening of all.

The strong eye contact makes me feel vulnerable, violated. Instinctively, I curl up against the bars, avert my eyes. I cast them down in trained submission, not knowing how to engage You as an equal. My heart pounds so hard I can feel it in my ears. Yet I am intoxicated. There is a deep excitement brimming against my anxiety.

I pull a couple of slow, deliberate breaths down into my weakened lungs; then I fortify myself, dig my courage up from beneath my fear to face You. I meet Your stare gingerly and do not find the cold, unfeeling expression of my training. Instead, a questioning paints Your features, an affection hiding in the corners.

I almost recoil again from the absence of my Master. Second after second, it remains startling and unsettling. You are here at the wrong time; You are looking at me the wrong way. I have not earned that look yet today. Yet I hold true. I do not move or breathe because I trust my Master above all things.

You keep Your eyes gently on me as the gears in the lock finally shift. The door creaks open and hangs ajar. The space around it suddenly seems like a chasm. Time stutters again as You do not reach through the door; You do not guide me out. You simply continue to kneel quietly beside my cage.

I place my palms tentatively flat along the blanket in front of the cage door. I feel the thin bars pressing into my skin. I feel the pressure of my fading weight in my shoulders, my elbows, my wrists. All my follicles are standing at attention in anticipation, in curiosity, in trepidation. I want to leap forward out of the cage to find out what You want, what You mean by all this. Yet I still find myself trembling and unmoving, frozen as my mind whirls.

You wait. Your body does not tense. Your breathing does not change. There is no impatience in Your air. You just wait.

I take another deep breath, with no care that the sound of it echoes against the dank concrete walls. I can see no reason to hide my apprehension, as if stifling an exhalation would be enough to do so. I feel my perplexity and bow my head as I wait for any signal from You.

"Stay with me," You say simply.

It is the first time I have heard Your voice in however many months or years spent in this room.

It is not gruff and unpracticed as I imagined. It is not deep and ominous as I imagined. It is not warbling psychotic as I imagined. It is plain, peaceful, as methodical as Your nature. Somehow, it just sounds like You.

I had spent endless hours imagining what You might sound like, what You might say to me. I would fantasize conversations and interactions between us. You would scream what a disappointment I was, or You would softly coo how pleased You were with me, but You would speak to me in the hours I was alone.

Your voice touching my ears, at last, is beautiful.

I close my eyes to let the sound truly resonate through my skull. I wrap my brain tightly around the waves and bury them in the safest, most trusted part of my memory. I secure the instance so that I can replay it again and again while I lay alone in the dark.

My eyes begin to tingle; my sinuses prickle. Such a rage of emotion roars up at Your words that I cannot even distinguish what it is. I am so lost at the sound of Your speech that I completely neglect to interpret Your words. As the shock dissipates over me and I quiver panting in the wake, I actually hear it.

Stay with me.

My uncertainty flashes again. *What does that mean? Stay with me? Is there any choice? Was there ever any choice? You never asked me anything. You only commanded nonverbally. What could You mean by stay with me?*

I look up to You with tears in my eyes, but You are no longer kneeling and waiting for me.

You walk out. I hear Your footsteps break heavily on the concrete as I watch Your figure grow smaller against the light and eventually disappear.

You have left me alone with my cage unlocked.

The light continues to pour into my room. The anticipated seconds pass, but the square does not collapse. I hear Your footsteps completely disappear. I wait and continue to wait. I feel my eyes shifting back and forth in my skull; I hear my breathing fall rapid and shallow. My pulse throbs in my palms still cemented to the blanket.

Nothing.

You have left me with my cell open.

What in the fuck?

You have left me with my cage still gaping open, with my room seized by light, with the outside world spilling in all around me and freedom licking at my heels. And a choice.

Stay with me.

A choice? What the fuck is a choice anymore? Maybe this is a test. All another test to see what picture graces my results page in the book.

Finally, it makes sense. Finally, I see the request; I translate the appeal laid at my feet by Your strangely questioning eyes.

For a second, out of dead habit, I see Lei's face. Her hair wraps around her face in the wind as she reaches down to grasp McAllister's dripping and slobbery tennis ball. She grimaces and laughs as it saturates her hand. I hear her awkward throaty laugh fade off into the distance. Some faint instinct struggles deep inside me, leaps into my heart and starts pounding. I feel adrenaline surge through my body, the same adrenaline that raged at the thought of shoving You aside and sprinting to my liberation.

Before all those dreams died in this room.

I smile, knowing You think I am complete, knowing I have made You proud, knowing that You know I am Yours. I am finally Your success. I will be the last in the book, and there will be no mutilated picture of my disobedient remains. I am Your realization.

Maybe I feel a breeze coming in through the door and swaying the door to my cage, or maybe I imagine it. I turn my back to the light and close my eyes, waiting for my Master to return.

About the Author

Colorado-bred writer, Christina Bergling knew she wanted to be an author in fourth grade.

In college, she pursued a professional writing degree and started publishing small scale. It all began with "How to Kill Yourself Slowly."

With the realities of paying bills, she started working as a technical writer and document manager, traveling to Iraq as a contractor and eventually becoming a trainer and software developer.

She avidly hosted multiple blogs on Iraq, bipolar, pregnancy, running. She continues to write on Fiery Pen: The Horror Writing of Christina Bergling and Z0mbie Turtle.

In 2015, she published two novellas. She is also featured in the horror collections *Collected Christmas Horror Shorts*, *Collected Easter Horror Shorts*, *Collected Halloween Horror Shorts*, and *Demonic Wildlife*. Her latest novel, *The Rest Will Come*, was released by Limitless Publishing in August 2017.

Bergling is a mother of two young children and lives with her family in Colorado Springs. She spends her non-writing time running, doing yoga and barre, belly dancing, taking pictures, traveling, and sucking all the marrow out of life.

christinabergling.com

facebook.com/chrstnabergling

@ChrstnaBergling

chrstnaberglingfierypen.wordpress.com

goodreads.com/author/show/11032481.Christina_Bergling

pinterest.com/chrstnabergling

instagram.com/fierypen/

amazon.com/author/christinabergling

The Waning

Depraved Desires: Volume 1

Desires.
We all have them, even if we won't admit it. Some are considered normal, and probably healthy. But what about the others?

Those haunting stirrings within that rail against societal norms and the bounds of decency?

Depraved Desires delves into the writhing depths of carnal appetites and sin, peeling back the veneer to reveal tales of wanton lust and supernatural depravity... The terrifying prospect of knife play; a cosmic liaison; a classy party that turned out to be more than a hired call girl ever expected; or when a sinister fantasy becomes reality - all will shock you.

Whether your desires drive you mad or your madness drives your desires, delving within these pages will take you to places where those itches live, the ones that demand to be scratched.

Depraved Desires: Volume 2

A dark and wonderfully stimulating collection of the disturbingly erotic from the very best authors in the business - all lovingly selected by the internationally renowned authoress Bonnie Capps.

Sixteen mouthwateringly delectable tales from: Duana Monroe, Jacob Mielke, Matt Payne, Ken Goldman, M.J. Sutton, D. Norfolk, Mawr Gorshin, J. Stanley, Tim J. Finn, Shane Porteous, J.L. Boekestein, Becky & Lee Narron, Marela Aryan Ballot, Becky Narron & J.L. Boekestein and Jennifer Lynne

The Pleasure Hunt

After meeting the mysterious *Dark Dance* on the casual encounters website, The Pleasure Hunters Club, *Sexy Cupid* finds himself enchanted by a enigmatic seductress – *Dark Dance*.

After experiencing bizarre, nightmarish visions during their first physical liaison, *Cupid* awakes on a bench somewhere in Louisville, unable to get the mystifying creature off his mind. As he begins to search both online and through the seedy streets of the city for her, he uncovers harrowing truths about the object of his obsession, truths which fill him with both indomitable dread and inexplicable love for her.

By the time *Cupid* begins to understand the terror he faces, the shackles on his soul are already too tight as the ancient monster has her talons dug well into his flesh.

Every time he is swept away to her world of Theia - the Moon Realm - she extracts and devours yet another piece of his very essence, and despite the merciless torment of his encounters with his obsession - and the warnings of, a menacing stranger - he presses on to find her, dragging himself deeper into her darkened realm.

Cupid soon finds that he may have but one opportunity to escape the demonic *Dark Dance*, but the bewitchment she has cast upon his heart may deter him from making a stand; with his soul about to slip down the gullet of the beast, *Cupid* has to make a decision before he is forever wrapped in the wicked thaumaturge's wings of eternal damnation.

The Cabin Sessions

A confronting, hard-hitting, dark psychological thriller told with acid wit. Themes of abuse are explored through minds distorted by fear and corrupted by hatred and delusion; this is a tale in which redemption is gained in unexpected ways.

It's Christmas Eve when hapless musician Adam Banks stands on the bridge over the river that cleaves the isolated village of Burton. A storm is rolling into the narrow mountain pass. He thinks of turning back. Instead, he resolves to fulfil his obligation to perform the guest spot at The Cabin Sessions. He should be looking forward to it, but fear stirs when he opens the door on the Cabin's incense-choked air

Philip Stone is already there, brooding. He observes with a ruthless eye the regulars, from sleazy barmaid Hannah Fisher, to old crone Cynthia Morgan. Meanwhile, Philip's sister, Eva, prepares to take a bath. It's a ritual - she's a breath holder. At twenty-eight, Eva has returned to Burton to finish the business of her past, as memories begin to surface concerning one fateful day by the river and the innocence of her beloved brother...

Surrogate for a Werewolf

A highly-charged erotic romance horror novel from the mistress of erotica...

Alyssa, 22 years old and still a virgin, replies to an ad' looking for a surrogate for the older, rich and powerful billionaire businessman, Brett Wolfram.
She is whisked away to his mysterious mansion in a far off land to be prepared for natural impregnation. There, Alyssa is indoctrinated into the seductive world of the werewolf, and becomes caught up in a centuries-old blood feud between Wolfram and his younger, incredibly handsome brother, Sal..

Alyssa is kidnapped and taken into the forest where she embraces her new status as a she-wolf, and finds herself falling in love - and lust - with the impossibly rugged, brooding Sal.

Brett Wolfram begins his quest to find Alyssa and return her to his mansion, his senses telling him that she is pregnant - but not if it is he, or his brother who is the father. Meanwhile, close behind him, those plotting his downfall begin their own hunt - their aim is to kill Wolfram and the heir to his empire...Alyssa's werewolf child.

A powerful, incredibly sensual story of sex, love and lycanthropes

The Big Book of Bootleg Horror 3:
By Invitation Only

A very, very special edition of our flagship anthology series - proceeds going to the awesome Alzheimer's charity *'Hilarity for Charity'*.

Only invited authors are featured - some of the biggest names in today's horror scene!

Authors contributing:

Jack Ketchum, Michael Bray, Jeff Strand, Chad Lutzke, Eddie Generous, Lance Tuck, Wade H. Garrett, Richard Chizmar and Billy Chizmar, James H Longmore, Jaap Boekestein, Iain Rob Wright, Michael McBride, Edward Lee, David Owain Hughes, Ray Garton & Benjamin Blake

**A HellBound Books LLC
Publication**

http://www.hellboundbookspublishing.com

Printed in the United States of America